PLEX

Philip Gross

SCHOLASTIC

*For Rosemary and Jonathan-
the best of both worlds.*

Scholastic Children's Books
Scholastic Publications Ltd,
7–9 Pratt Street, London NW1 0AE

Scholastic Inc.,
555 Broadway, New York, NY 10012–3999, USA

Scholastic Canada Ltd,
123 Newkirk Road, Richmond Hill,
Ontario, Canada, L4C 3G5

Ashton Scholastic Pty Ltd,
PO Box 579, Gosford, New South Wales,
Australia

Ashton Scholastic Ltd,
Private Bag 92801, Penrose, Auckland
New Zealand

First published by Scholastic Children's Books 1994
Copyright © Philip Gross 1994

ISBN 0 590 54176 5

Typeset by Create Publishing Services Ltd, Bath, Avon
Printed in England by Clays Ltd, St Ives plc

10 9 8 7 6 5 4 3 2 1

1.

We're talking monsters. I don't just mean *big* things – not like "MONSTER PRIZES TO BE WON". I don't even mean *huge*. I mean things so weird that it's a wonder they're allowed to *be* at all.

Skinner's shop seemed a good place to look. Not to go in. You needed a year or two of pocket money to buy anything in there, because everything was rare. If you wanted a gerbil or a goldfish you'd go down to Fur 'n' Feathers in the precinct, or out of town to World of Pets. The people who found their way round under the railway bridge to Skinner's Exotics were people looking for something out of the ordinary.

There weren't many of them. One little nothingy man came out as I stood by the window. He had his raincoat collar up and his head down. I could see the bald patch on top, with one long strand of hair greased down over it from the side. He looked like someone come for dirty videos, not pets. He hurried past, and didn't look at me.

I went on peering in the window. It was so dirty I had to get close. One glass tank said GILA MONSTER but the creature in it didn't look monstrous to me: a big lizard, that's all, with a fat stumpy tail. It looked like something stuffed, a bit too much. The only thing moving in the cage was a daddy-long-legs frying itself one leg at a time on the lightbulb. The monster-that-wasn't just stood on its stone in its miniature desert, staring nowhere, and I couldn't even see it blink. The Great Horned Toad in the next tank sounded promising, but seemed to be out for lunch. I looked from tank to cage to tank. A Bird-eating Spider squatted like a weight-lifter just about to lift, but nothing happened. Only the Axolotl looked me in the eye.

It was pudgy and pink, like something half-made and half-baked, and it had tiny sunk-in eyes. It was basically newt, with feathery gills that stuck out where ears might have been, like bonsai bushes. It trod water dreamily towards me, and I wondered how anything could look so disgustingly new-born *and* so very old. I was staring so hard I didn't realize, not till I noticed that feeling you get, that something, someone else was watching me.

Between the Axolotl's tank and the next cage, not an arm's reach away, there was a human face. It had very pale eyes and no lashes to speak of. When I jumped it didn't move at all, and neither could I, with those eyes on me. If anything, they narrowed slightly. I longed for him to tap the glass and mouth *Hop it*, so I could run away. It was a bottom-heavy face, more chin than anything else, as though the whole thing had sagged when it wasn't quite set. The hair was cropped fiercely and the skin was tanned in a way that didn't seem likely for England, let alone our end of town.

This was all in that first long look. Then he blinked, rather slowly, like cats do. With the ghost of a nod, his eyes still on me, Skinner very slightly smiled. For a moment the window was a glass tank and I was one of his exotic specimens. Then there was a whine and a thudding behind me as an InterCity shook the bridge. Someone's eyes wavered, his or mine, and I was free. I turned and walked, then walked faster, then walked very fast, for home.

I was still out of breath when Mum opened the door. "You're back," she said, then: "What's wrong?" The Step looked up through the banisters. His name's Jeff – my Stepdad but I call him the Step, or sometimes the Door-step, when he lets Mum walk all over him. He had his Black & Decker in his hand and there was a mist of wood dust in the air. He's always *sanding something down*. Sand anything down far enough, you'll come to good wood underneath: that's what the Step believes. He'd sand down the city if he could.

"Oy, oy," he said. "You been jogging?"

I gave them an all-purpose grin and slipped past him, clattering up the bare stairs, quickly, so I wouldn't have to answer Mum's "What's wrong?" How could I, when I didn't know?

2.

Extracts from the *Journal of The Association For The Study Of Unthinkable Animals*

THE HYPERVELOCIPOD *(popularly known as Einstein's Cheetah)*

An unfortunate mutation caused by a misunderstanding of Einstein's Theory of Relativity, which states that the nearer a body gets to the speed of light, the smaller it becomes . . .

(That's true, by the way. I read books.)

Unlike most animals, which need more food the faster they run, this creature needs less. On a good day it can actually exceed the speed of light and pass through the state of having no mass into one of having less than nothing. Thus it needs less than no food and spends its time collecting food to feed its prey. The effort exhausts it and renders the world safe from what would otherwise have been a most dangerous predator.

Mad? Me? I know, I know. When Mum finds me writing things like that, she gets worried, and when she's worried she gets angry. So I keep it out of sight.

I've always made things up. When I was four I couldn't sleep. I used to lie in bed with my little night-light on, making hand-shadows on the wall. I used to call out at first, till Mum or Dad came in with *"One more sound from you and ..."* I shut up.

I couldn't do people, of course, so all my stories were about animals. Snakes were easy. Wolves, too, specially when they howled. Then there were all the other creatures I invented, or found my hands doing by chance. Monsters. Some were scary, but they were *my* monsters. I was almost sorry when the dawn came up and the shadows got fainter and fainter, like ghosts, till all my animals were gone.

I don't need night-lights now. I do it in my head. Or I write it in my Unthinkable Animals notebook. That night after I'd run home from Skinner's Exotics, I dreamed overtime. I slept in late so I could dream some more, then I got out my notebook. Now I snapped it shut and slipped it under the bed. It was thirsty work, keeping up with Einstein's Cheetah, and I needed a quick glass of milk. I crept downstairs.

The sanding-down had stopped. Sometimes it's that Black & Decker whine, sometimes it's sandpaper and elbow grease, scrape, scrape, scrape, like a column of soldier ants eating their way through the house. But it had stopped. I was almost in the breakfast room before I heard their voices. Mum's was very quiet.

"He ought to *get out* more. He ought to have friends."

The Step shrugged. "Give him time. You know Todd ..."

"Yes, I think I probably do." Her voice, still quiet, went saw-edged. "I *am* his mother."

"Sorry," he mumbled into his Sixties moustache. "I just meant: don't worry so much ... let him be."

"*Let him be*? I haven't seen him all day. He's been up in that room since breakfast. It's not healthy, Jeff. What does he *do* up there?"

"The kid's on holiday. Probably stuck in a good book."

Mum banged her mug down so hard that the coffee splashed out on the stripped-pine table. It would mark. She'd told me so often enough. "*Good book*! You've seen the stuff he reads. It makes me sick."

"All the kids read horror these days. You've seen it at school."

"I've seen it. Have *you*? Have you *read* one of those things?" She brushed the slopped coffee aside, hard. "Jeff, I've tried to bring him up on *good books*. I don't mean Topsy and Tim. I mean lively, exciting ... and he used to love it. You don't know how he's changed."

That was mean. Of course he wouldn't know. Twelve months ago, he wasn't there. He was just Mum's friend from school, Jeff, not our Step. He picked up a piece of sandpaper thoughtfully.

"Jan, it takes time. If you didn't go on at him ... "

"Me? *Go on*? If you *talked* to him once in a while ... "

"That's not fair ... "

I was leaning in the doorway. That was me they were scrapping about. And they hadn't even noticed I was standing there. So I got out, like Mum said. I slammed the front door. That felt good. The trouble was – and this dawned on me just seconds afterwards – that they were in the house, and I was outside in the street.

3.

I stared at the front door, hating it. If you could see it you'd hate it too. Stripped and varnished, with a lion's head knocker in bronze. In a street like that it was like shouting: *Here, you peasants, look at us!*

For a minute I thought the door would fly open and Mum would be standing there, blazing. But no. I could hear their voices through it. I could almost make out what they said. The new letter box slit was a smug little smile that said: my lips are sealed. That was when I thought: I'm running away.

It made me laugh. I mean, where would I go? I didn't know a soul within miles. I didn't know Sly then, of course. If this had been home – old home, that is, before the move, before Mum realized she's *never* liked the country, all those years – I'd have slipped down the woods. But here? At the top of the street you could hear the Inner Ring Road. At the bottom was waste ground, the warehouses, then the canal. I went that way.

The warehouses were two huge square silhouettes. Against the orange sky you could see a kind of catwalk between them, several storeys up. Torn sheets of corrugated iron dangled from it, squeaking in the wind. The place was fenced off. I pressed my face close, till I could feel the cool wire on my cheeks.

GUARD DOGS ON PATROL ... The sign showed an Alsatian, grinning. I'd never seen a dog there, but some nights I'd heard one yelping and yowling. That's what I thought, then, anyway.

There were kids on the gravel, just inside the wire – kids of my age, plus or minus a couple of years. They were the kids from round here, ones I kept on seeing in the street, ones who went to the local school that Mum thought wasn't good enough for me. They turned, in a clump, and stared at me. Then one of the big ones laughed. It's all right, it's all right, I told myself, backing away. There's a ten-foot fence between them and me. Then I thought: they got in there somehow, so they can get out. I almost started to run. Run where? Not home. No, I would show them all – Mum, the Step, the jeering kids. I turned on my heel and strode the other way.

They'd lost interest already. They were back in their clump, lighting up. I walked fast, gritting my teeth till they hurt. I saw myself, in gorgeous detail, landing a neat punch in the big kid's face. I saw him stumbling backwards, with handfuls of blood. *Who's next?* I was saying, real soft and deadly. All this with the zoom-lens and slow-mo effects you get from total fantasy. Round the corner was an iron foot-bridge like a criss-cross cage. No-one coming. No-one anywhere. Beyond the canal was the waste reclamation plant, where bundles of shredded paper rose up in a shaggy white cliff. There was the car-crushers' yard, and . . . well, a lot of things like that.

I leaned on a girder, breathing hard and gazing down into the water. It didn't flow. Now and then something gulped from a pipe in the wall. Once a water-rat launched in from somewhere. In its bow-wave, the reflections of the warehouses were oily squiggles. I stared but I wasn't really looking. If I'd have *known* this was the start of something . . . But you don't do you?

You know that moment when you've been blazing inside, with the way things aren't fair, families in particular, then suddenly the fire goes out and everything just tastes like ashes. That's when it happened. Splash.

The warehouses went five, six, seven storeys up – a hundred windows, all barred and shuttered, and whatever it was could have come from any of them. It wasn't a dead weight. Not like a body, concrete overcoats and that stuff. No, this splashed down slower, with a slapping, flapping sound. Black ripples clucked against the girders of the footbridge underneath my feet. I blinked and tried to focus on a dark thing that had fallen. It was struggling. It was going down.

It's a wonder that anything ever *sinks* in that canal. It's silting up – weed, mud and things you don't look at too close, that float downstream and settle. No-one's used it for years, not up this far. Down by the Docks it's different – all sailboards, pleasure cruises, you know the kind of stuff. Warehouses glossied up into flats and offices: PRESTIGE DEVELOPMENT . . . Up here, they let them rot.

The thing got a wing out – glistening, more like leather than feathers, then fell back. It was drowning inch by inch. Its head jerked backwards, snapping for air, long jaws clacking shut and open . . . then it went down. The light and dark went crazy on the surface; waves started slapping the wall. Just as the head was sucked under I heard . . . What? It might have been a screech of brakes on the ring road, but it seemed to come from the warehouse above me – a faint, high, wailing sort of scream.

4.

You think I was dreaming? I was wide awake. So what if it couldn't be true? All the "real" things of my life, like Mum and Dad, bad times, the move, the Step, the new house, here, they were the dream, the kind of dream you wake up tired from. This was like being *awake*. This was real.

I closed my eyes and I could see it: a shape like something on a coat of arms, a gryphon or a wyvern, one of those pick 'n' mix monsters. Snout like a crocodile, wings like a bat ... go on, say it: *dragon*. I'd read books with dragons in, I'd been through the fantasy thing, oh, years ago. It didn't fit, not *here*. The canal was still again. A train rattled the steel bridge just downstream. Somewhere a siren – fire, police or ambulance? – was going somewhere fast.

I imagined myself running through the front door. "Mum, I'm back. Guess what? I saw a dragon!" It wasn't a joke. It was unthinkable. "Don't be silly," she'd say, with that pinch of her lips. Then she'd worry. "I'm worried about Todd. Jeff, listen. This is serious. Do you know what he said?"

If I was her, I'd worry. Wouldn't you? My age, you're meant to be into sports and trainers. You're meant to hang around with friends, not sit and read alone. Sit, read, then put down the book and think: *what if ...* ?

When you're a little kid it's easy. Make up stories, have imaginary friends ... people think it's cute. And when you're an adult, well, one in a million, you might get to be a film director or a writer. Or an inventor – that would be best: not making up stories or pictures but real things, large as life.

Oh yeah, you say, Professor Branestawm? Leave off. I get enough of that at school. When I say real *things* I mean it. I've read about genetic engineering, stuff that sounds like magic but it's true. I've read *Frankenstein* too. The real book, that is, not the cartoon version. Lots of people don't know that Frankenstein is the inventor. The monster's got no name. And *it's* the hero, not him. It's sort of sad and lonely, made of bits and pieces, no place for it in the world. That's what makes it mad.

I headed home. I'd stopped running away. The game was over. It seemed rather silly, all of a sudden. No, I had some serious thinking to do, and there was only one place for that: upstairs in my room. I came round the bend in the path, and stopped. I'd forgotten the kids on the waste ground. There they were. They didn't look so cool now, or so big. They were squeezing through a low hole in the fence, jostling to be first. As each one pushed through they set off down the path towards the houses, not exactly running – sort of sauntering very fast, to show they weren't scared. All but one.

The last one through was smaller than the others. He or she looked like no shape at all, just a wobbly black bundle trapped under the wire. As I watched it, it wriggled and stretched. Then a head lifted up at one end, looked down the path where the others were vanishing, and shouted something really foul.

I waited. It wriggled and tugged and the bundle

stretched further. Next time it called it sounded weaker, sort of hopeless. "Wait for me."

I came up, not too close. Most of what I could see was an enormous floppy pullover, black but smeared with mud and grass. It was snagged on the sharp wire, and each tug pulled it tighter, like a sheep caught in a thornbush. "Keep still," I said.

"What?" The head turned suddenly my way, twitched a tangle of hair back and stared at me. It was, I was almost sure, a girl. "Get me out of here," she said, as if it was my fault. She tugged again, so another twist of the pullover hooked on the wire.

"Relax." I was squatting beside her now. "Back a bit . . . there." With a last little rip and unravelling, she squirmed free and struggled to her feet. We faced each other for a moment. I thought she was going to say *Thank You*. I was wrong.

"Did you hear it?" I said. She looked away. She *had*, I knew it. "That noise," I said. "You . . . the others, they were running away. Did you see anything?"

"Don't know what you're talking about." She glanced at the warehouse. She scowled. "It's all stories. Don't believe it. Kids' stuff. OK?" She looked up the path where her mates had gone and left her. "Ask them," she muttered.

"Wait a minute. What . . . ?" I started, but she had turned her back and was off up the path without another look at me.

5.

When I got back home, Mum didn't say a thing. She looked baggy round the eyes, and the Step was nowhere in sight. Mum didn't even call after me when I went upstairs.

THE SHTUMBAT (or Hushmugger)

The octopus uses ink, the skunk its smell; the shtumbat uses the most powerful form of silence known to nature. One squirt, and predators become completely tongue-tied and confused. The paralysing force of this silence comes from the shtumbat's enormous ears. In earliest times it was teased without mercy by other, small-eared life-forms. In self-defence the shtumbat evolved the ability to use its ears like vacuum cleaners, sucking up sound faster than anything could make it, thus sparing itself a lot of embarrassment.

The Association For The Study of Unthinkable Animals convened an emergency meeting. I'm the only member, so it didn't take much organizing. I tried again to make some sense of what I'd seen.

"*A prodigy, a marvel . . . A malformed animal or plant . . . An imaginary animal, partly brute and partly human, or compounded from two or more animal forms . . .*" That's what the dictionary said. *Monster.* A thing made out of parts that didn't fit.

Feet on the landing, the click of a door: Mum was creeping

up to bed. *Families are monsters*, I thought, and that made me smile. Imagine Mum and Dad, or Mum and the Step: different life-forms grafted together somehow. Might as well be brought up by a centaur or a basilisk.

I tried to sketch what I'd seen from the footbridge, but nothing looked right. I just couldn't catch the way it had moved – heavy, clumsy but fighting. Most of all I couldn't catch that sound – the cry of something that had cried for the monster far off, out of sight. I fell asleep that night with pictures of dark water and the warehouse, and I didn't have good dreams.

Next morning was wet, but I did what I was told. I got out. Mum was right: if I went on like this all holiday, just hanging round the house, someone was going to go bananas.

The bus shelter was one of those perspex affairs with posters in it, except who wants to advertise in an area like this? So it looked like a fish tank or a display case in a museum. There was one exhibit: *Girl, Smoking*. Her black pullover bagged around her, with a ripped bit dangling. Her hair hung down and forward, with barely a parting to let the fag end in and out. The steady rhythm – in, out, puff, puff – stopped. She looked at me.

"What did you mean, last night?" I said. "*It's all stories*? What?"

There was a slight shrug underneath the hair.

"Tell me," I said. "I *like* stories."

"You're weird," she said.

"Weird? ... " I said. *"Eerie. Supernatural. Uncanny.* Good word!"

"Weird," she repeated. "Posh. You talk like a book."

"That's good."

"Good. Why?"

"Because I'm going to the library." No reply. "Do you want to know why?" She shrugged. I went on. "Because I want a picture of a pterodactyl. You know what a ptero-dactyl is?"

"'Course I do." She snapped. "D'you think I'm stupid?" The movement flounced her hair aside so we were face to face. Hers was flattish and wide. You couldn't say *pretty*. Even her mother couldn't have called her that. Her eyes were green.

"People like you ... " she went on. "People like you and your darling Mummy and her bloke and your hanging baskets and your Greenpeace stickers, you move in and think you own the place. And you don't know a thing about this place. Not a thing."

As she spoke, the little pendants round her neck danced on their leather thongs. There was a skull. A crystal. And ...

"What's that?" I said. "Is it real?"

"It's real, OK." She touched the tight-curled scaley claw. "Finders keepers. You want one, you go down the Werehouse and look for your own."

"*Were*-house?"

"You heard what I said."

A snub yellow bus, that might have been mine, pulled in. Neither of us moved. "Why were your mates in such a hurry to get out of there last night? You saw something, didn't

you?" No answer. "You know why I'm talking about ptero-
dactyls ... "

"You missed your bus," she said. "Better start
walking."

"Weren't you waiting? Where's your mates?"

She was back inside the folds of hair. "Down the Pool,"
she said. "They'll be back soon. You'd better be gone when
they do."

"Swimming? Nice. Why aren't you with them?"

She dropped the last crumb of her cigarette and crushed
it with her trainer till it was only a smear. "I just don't like it.
OK?"

"Sorry," I said. "I'm Todd. You?"

"Sly."

"Pardon?"

"Short for Sally-Ann. Everybody calls me Sly." There
was a pause. The rain crackled on the perspex all around us.
"Were-house. Like in werewolf, see? A joke. All the kids
know, though the grown-ups don't." She stepped out in the
rain. "That's where your Terror-thingy came from," she
said over her shoulder. "Now are you satisfied?"

6 .

NO ADMITTANCE, said a rusty notice. *UNSAFE STRUCTURE. DANGER OF COLLAPSE.*

The warehouse was a fortress. Barred windows and a small door reinforced with steel. Boatloads of tobacco used to be unloaded here, with the Excise men watching; unloaded and slammed under lock and key, in bond.

A prison . . . It was getting dark. It might be summer but it looked like November, with clouds low enough to blur the tops of the high-rise towers downtown. We don't get horizons here at the best of times. That night the grey closed in till the warehouse seemed to be the only solid thing.

I wiped my glasses one last time, and gave up. The tissue in my pocket was a cold dumpling. I pulled up my anorak hood, took one glance round – who'd be out on an evening like this? – and ducked down where I'd seen the kids creeping out the other night.

We used to have obstacle courses at school. The only times I wasn't last were when everyone else slowed down to laugh at me. "Never known a boy with so many knees and elbows," Mister Smart used to say. I eased myself into the mud and wriggled. There was a rip; something bit at my sleeve. I tugged; the wire twanged back. I straightened up and waited for the howl. (Do guard dogs howl?) Nothing happened. I was inside.

Suddenly I felt stupid. Here I was, wet to my socks, with

mud all over, creeping upon an empty building. Of course it was empty. Those security signs are just bluff, everybody knows that. There were brambles ten feet high, and buddleia bushes cracking up the tarmac. It was waste ground, and had been for years.

Up close, the windows had a no-way look. The shutters were steel, and closed without a chink. They looked airtight. The place made me think of a submarine. There might be processed air in there, an artificial climate, like a space craft that could stay in orbit years and years and years. I turned back, scuffing the gravel. No need to be quiet. There was no-one, no risk, no adventure, no point being here at all. That's when I saw the tyre tracks at my feet.

They were deep and chunky – treads like a big van or jeep. The patch of mud was filling up with rain and I couldn't see much, but the tyre-cuts were sharp-edged; they couldn't have been old. And there, by the rusty wire gate that was almost hidden by the brambles, there they were again. I stared at that gate for a while before I noticed one small thing. The padlock that held the long steel bar in place was on *this* side, the inside of the wire.

"You again," said a voice.

As I jerked round, the rain caught me straight in the face and made my glasses smeary. All I could see was a shape. It laughed. "What're you doing out on a night like this?"

"Sly! What am *I* doing out? What are *you*?"

"Just passing."

"Don't believe you."

"I saw you creeping down here, and I thought ..."

"Thought what?"

"I thought: *He'll get himself in trouble.*"

"Don't believe you. You wouldn't have come ... just for me."

"Suit yourself. Don't believe me. No-one else does." There was something in her voice that made me wipe my glasses and look close, though I still couldn't see.

"We can't talk here," I said. "It's sheltered over there." She looked at the warehouse. She shook her head. "It's OK," I said. "I've looked round. It's locked up, empty ..." She shook her head again.

"Sly," I said, once we were out of the rain between the buildings. "What do you know?"

Big drips splattered down out of a broken drainpipe just over our heads. Every now and then a big gust made the catwalk squeak. Sly was shivering; that pullover of hers was all silvery with rain. "Sorry about yesterday," she said. "I was a cow."

We looked at each other with something like a smile.

"This place ... " I said. "What are these stories you don't want to talk about? Tell me."

7 .

Sly glanced upwards at the warehouse walls. They seemed to close above our head. She was quite a bit shorter than me; it was the first time I'd noticed that. She was probably younger, too.

"Stories," she said. "You know, the kind kids scare each other with. Like that lane there's called Dead Dog Lane."

"Start with that," I said.

"Stupid stuff. Several cats and dogs went missing ... "

So this was the big mystery? We'd lost Pushkin (Mum's idea, *Pushkin*, not mine) just after we moved in here. Big soft thing, he spent a week whining around the house – couldn't go out in the yard because one of the next-door cats would be down off the wall and scrag him, just like that. I think he got it into his pea-brain to walk home, fifty miles, and that was that.

"So?" I said.

"One night Mrs Barker's youngest ran home screaming her head off. Said she'd found a dead dog in the lane."

"Dogs get run over. Happens all the time."

"No, listen. What she said was ... well, that the dog was sort of ... changed. It had her Missy's face."

The gutter made a choking noise. Drip, drip.

"Missy?"

"Missy was her cat. She lost it a few days before. I know, she's just little, this kid, but ... it was the way she said it."

She gave a shudder like a wet dog. Drops sprayed off her. "No, it's like you said. Things get run over. Probably mashed up its head a bit. I've seen worse. It was gone when they went back, anyway."

I tried a different angle. "There's a van or something comes in here."

She shook her head. "Nah. Nothing parks here. I'd have noticed."

When I told her about the tyre tracks she didn't speak for quite some time. "Well," she said. "You aren't such a fool as you look."

"Someone *lives* here," I said. "Could be in there now."

"You said it was empty." Now she wasn't bluffing. She was scared. "It's all locked up."

"Locked? Sure. What if it's locked *from the inside*?"

Crack. We both looked up. The sound of the corrugated sheeting was suddenly louder, but there was no wind. Something had banged, like a door slamming open, and high above our heads was a sharp urgent whimpering as if a live thing was perched on the edge. And when we looked harder, that was what it was.

A head poked over the catwalk. It was just a silhouette, with ears. That was all I noticed: ears. It looked straight at us; I froze, waiting for the barking. But it didn't seem to see. Then it lifted its head up. It looked out over the waste ground and over the fence, out into the distance. It might have been sniffing the wind, except it didn't seem to have a snout. There was that whimpering again.

"Guard dog!" I said.

Sly whispered, "That's no dog."

"Pekinese?" I said feebly. But the head had twitched, alert. If its eyes weren't too sharp, it could certainly hear. The movement made the catwalk wobble. There was a shuddering all along the bridge. *UNSAFE STRUCTURE* ... Sly and I had both backed away fast, but from the corner of the building we looked back.

Whatever it was, we could see it more in profile now. It was moving in rubbery jolts, like a thing in a sack. It kept very low and was dragging something heavy that slewed from side to side like an articulated lorry on black ice. It was a tail. With a dangerous heave it lashed out over the edge and round, so the creature was backing out onto the catwalk. The snuffling sound went up a pitch or two, as the figure of a man appeared.

He was crouching, I could see that, reaching out and down. It was like the Doorstep on the evening Pushkin vanished, creeping out in the yard with a saucer of milk and calling in a baby-talking voice. *Pushkin. Pushkin.* I used to cringe in the kitchen: the neighbours would hear. Now there was a man up there, four storeys up, in the same silly posture, in a place nobody ought to be.

The two shapes were still now. Sometimes the man would inch forward, almost on hands and knees, and the other would shrink back; the whole house of cards would sway; they would freeze. Then the man made a pounce. The catwalk shuddered with the struggle. The long tail lashed, and a sheet of corrugated iron peeled off its nails. Sly and I ducked as it crashed. When we looked back there was nothing up there. Just for a moment, before a door slammed, the squealing went on, getting higher and higher till it was almost out of human hearing. I had heard that sound before, from the footbridge that night: a wailing, almost bat-pitch scream.

8.

Even when we were out in the lane and round the corner, out of sight, it was a while before we spoke. "That was no kind of dog," Sly said again.

"Why would anybody want to keep a – whatever it was – in a place like that?"

Sly looked at me hard. "I've heard about experiments. Putting stuff in rabbits' eyes. Cutting things up alive."

"Vivisection," I said.

"I know," she said. "I'm not stupid." Her eyes went narrow. "If that's what they're doing in there ... I'll kill them. I'll cut bits off them, whoever they are."

She meant it. "I like animals, too," I said, faintly. She looked at me with scorn.

"Animals are better than people," she said. "People are a load of rubbish." She wasn't slow and dumpy now. She was wild. "What shall we do?" I said.

"Let's burn it down," she said.

"Wait a minute. We don't know ... I mean, there's no proof ... "

She spat in the mud. She scared me. "I know," I said. "Let's watch for the van."

"Good," she said quietly. "That's a good move."

"Maybe your mates could help."

"Not them. They haven't got the bottle. And they won't like you."

"Sorry for living," I said.

"They just don't like outsiders. Specially not people like your mum."

"I can't help her," I said, and meant it.

"'Course not. Sorry. Friends?" She fished inside her sweater. "Have a fag."

I had just reached the *do-you-know-what-it-does-to-your-lungs . . . if-you-could-see-the-tar* . . . bit when I noticed she'd gone hard again. "That's what I mean. Bet your mum says that. Do-gooders." I swallowed hard.

"Sorry. It was nice of you to offer. I didn't mean . . . "

"I know, I know. And you're right, too. Wish I didn't smoke. But you've got to, with the others. You're a snob if you don't. That's the way it is."

"Shall I take one?" I said. "Maybe try it later?" If I threw it away, she needn't know.

"Nah, don't."

We stood for a moment. "What happens now?" I said.

"I'll watch. When I see the van, I'll let you know."

"OK. We're at number . . . "

"I know where you live," she said. "So does everybody in the street. Look, in a place like this, you'd be amazed what people know." I was just about to say *What?* when she touched me for the first time. She grabbed me by the anorak sleeve and yanked me back into the bush beside the path. "Hey . . . " I said. "Shut up," she said through gritted teeth.

There was a thud, thud, coming down the lane. Closer. I could hear it panting hard. Her grip tightened, daring me to move. I held my breath. Something that smelt of hot sweat whacked past. Its bristling head was thrust forward so hard that veins bulged in its neck. It wore serious trainers and a khaki vest and shorts.

"Him!" she said. "Just for a moment then I thought . . ." She grinned. Then stopped. I wasn't grinning. "Come on," she said. "Only a jogger."

"Do you know that man?"

"He comes round here running. Doing press-ups on the grass, martial arts moves, that kind of thing. He looks like a commando. He's a fitness nut." She looked the way he'd gone. "Mind you, I wouldn't say that to his face. I reckon he's really hard, no joke." She looked back. "Why? Do *you* know him? Friend of yours?"

I shook my head. "I've seen him in a shop, that's all." But I still couldn't smile. Somehow I didn't like the idea of Skinner coming quite this close to home.

9.

I can't draw to save my life. I took my tenth sheet of paper, closed my eyes and tried to see it again. I could manage the buildings, and the catwalk, even the low clouds blowing by behind, but the creature wouldn't come. I got the outline of the man OK, and I felt a bit like him, trying to coax something to come a step nearer so that I could see it clearly. But everything I drew looked wrong.

A bit like a lizard, it was, especially that heavy lashing tail, as long as the body again. But where there should have been a snout to balance it, there was a flat piggy face. And those ears. Bat's ears ... I scowled at my last try at drawing it, and scratched it out. As I scrawled I remembered how it moved: jerky and to and fro, like that. It felt how it would feel: heavy and rubbery, quivering as it jerked and backed away.

The door snicked open. Mum came in, geared up to say something, then she saw the drawing spread out on the floor. "Todd? What's all this?"

"You didn't knock." I knew this scene. We've had it fifty times before.

"What's the point? You never answer when I do."

I scraped up the pictures in a hurry. I felt like a kid in a playgroup: *Look Mummy what I drawed*. The creatures looked clumsy and childish and weird, and I could have sworn they winced as I crumpled them up, just like the thing at the warehouse had done. She glanced at them as though they smelt bad. "You've got to grow up," she said. "You could at least draw something *real*." She held out an envelope. "This came through the door."

It looked like a gas bill. But there was my name, spelt wrong – TOD – in felt-penned letters on the front. It was sellotaped shut. "Thanks," I said and waited for Mum to go. She didn't.

"I saw the girl who brought it. Is she . . . " Mum paused, " . . . a friend of yours?"

I don't know why I blushed. I could imagine Mum at the window, taking Sly in at one glance. She's good at that. She's quick on accents, little mannerisms, things like that. I've heard her with her friends when they've had a glass or two of wine. She can be very funny and she always says "I shouldn't really, but . . . " so you can't really mind.

I imagined her noticing Sly's slouchy way of standing, that horrible sweater and the way she drags her hair about. She'd have noticed she's not very pretty and she's got spots and somehow doesn't look too bright. I imagined her thinking (but not saying): *not our type*.

You must say this for Mum: she's forty but she can pass for ten years younger, on a good day. All the women in the street looked old. Even the teenage ones, just left school, with a couple of babies; they looked as if they'd had one rave-up party and now it was the morning-after from here on.

I remembered the woman I'd seen that morning on the way back from the shops. She was wide as a bus, her and her Tesco bags. I had to scoot off the pavement and she barged right past, with a couple of snotty toddlers behind her. She might have been Sly's mother. That same jaw, that face.

A friend of yours? I shook my head hard and tried to smile but it went all crooked. I put the letter on my desk and left it there till Mum had gone.

DEAR TOD. HOPE YOU HAVENT FORGOTEN. IM STILL LOOKING OUT. BE REDDY TO HELP WEN I GIVE YOU THE CALL. YOU SAYED YOU WOUD. YOUD BETTER. SLY.

I shuddered. Then I crumpled it up small. Then I opened it out again, tore it up into several pieces and crumpled each of those. I imagined Mum finding it, frowning at the spelling, then turning to me: "What's *this* all about then?"

I thought of Skinner, jogging. The smell of his sweat. And I thought of the thing on the catwalk. And the monster drowned in the canal, its bones down in the mud. And the cry of the thing that cried out when it died. How could I start to tell Mum anything? How *could* she understand?

I crashed on the bed and picked up the thickest library book I could find. A couple of visits to the local branch, and I'd nearly finished their section on the paranormal. Did you know, they say people can spontaneously combust? *Eh?* came Sly's voice. (What was it doing lodged in my mind?) *Say it in English.*

One day, without warning, they just go up in flames.

1 0 .

When it happened it happened so fast I didn't have time to say *No*. There'd been a week or so of nothing. I'd walked down to the warehouses a few times, but there wasn't a sign. That was afternoons, mostly. If I'd been out after dark I knew what Mum would've thought. She'd have thought: *that girl* . . . I couldn't face that somehow. So I read books in the evenings, till I fell asleep.

Crack. I opened my eyes and looked round. The glowing hands on the alarm clock said midnight. Crack – at the window – again. I stuck my head under the curtains. There was something on the garden wall. I say *garden* – it's only a yard, though the Doorstep's started doing clever things with flowers in chimney pots. But the thing on the wall was either the biggest cat ever or this was it. Action.

I slid the sash up a crack and stuck out my head. "Sly?"

I could see she was dead relieved that she'd got the right house. *Ssssh*! she mimed, then, *Come on. Out here. Quick.*

It was easier than you'd think, climbing along the backyard wall. Some dogs barked a bit inside one house, but no-one looked out. That was all. I mean, it was so easy you wonder why people don't do it more often. Then again, maybe they do. But not people like me. You just don't think of it – trespassing, breaking and entering almost – do you? Sly did, though.

"What's going on?" We were down by the warehouse fence. I'd been sweating at first. Now I noticed that the clothes I'd slipped on weren't that warm. It was very dark and the street seemed a long way back. The no-man's-land of the car dump rose like mountains miles away.

"The van," Sly said. "Just after dark."

"Why didn't you tell me?"

"How? Knock on the door? I saw your Mum the other day and the look she gave me ... you didn't tell her anything, did you?"

"Never! What about the van?"

"I was right." Up close, she had a slight mushroomy unwashed smell. That, and the smoke and chewing gum. "It looked like any old clapped-out van, except for the bars. There were bars. And ... "

There was a flicker of bluish lighting, then faint hollow thunder from the railway bridge. The lights of the InterCity to nowhere in particular flickered through the girders. Arc-flashes scuffed from its wheels. The dogs that had barked at us started up again.

"And I swear there was a face ... looking out through the bars."

"Guard dog?"

She rattled my sleeve. "I said: *face*. I thought it was a kid at first. It was some kind of monkey."

"We should tell the police."

She snorted. "Two things. One: vivisection isn't against the law. It happens all over. No-one gets done for it. Two: you call in the police and no-one in this place'll speak to you again. And that includes me."

Something squeaked in the brambles. I'd never been out this late here. You'd think in the city, in a dead bit like this, there'd be nothing happening at night. You've got to be out in it and really still, then you notice these little sounds everywhere. The things that snuffle, things that yelp or shriek. Over by the paper-mountain there was something that sounded like a hammer hitting a twanging metal plate. It must have been alive, though, because another answered it.

"Well then? What do we do?"

"We go in."

"Go in? But we can't. It's private."

She didn't laugh out loud, but I could see her teeth in the dark. "I mean ... " I said, "it's locked. And even if we could get in, what would we do?"

"Get proof. That's a start. Then ... " She gritted her teeth again. "Then we'll see."

I didn't want to sound stupid. I just wished I was back home in bed. "There's no way in," I said. "I looked, remember?"

"An expert, are you?" She showed her teeth again. "I've been nosing round this week. I reckon there's an easy one round the side there. Couldn't do it alone, but with you ...? A piece of cake."

11.

A piece of cake. I should have known that Sly would be right about that sort of thing. Breaking and entering, I mean. She stalked round that building like someone who knew exactly what to look for. "Do you do this often?" I said. She gave me a withering look. I didn't ask again.

The hatch was just under the pulley housing, and there was this crack – *UNSAFE STRUCTURE*, all right – just wide enough for a toecap. I'd never have spotted it. I wouldn't have guessed that the sheet of rotting galvanized iron would give just enough, or that Sly, not the slimmest of kids, could shrink through the gap like a cat.

"Give me a leg up." She planted a boot in my hands and I staggered, but it was enough. She got a hand up on the hatch and hung for a moment like a dead weight. Then she scrabbled for a foothold, found it and went aping up. Her bottom half thrashed about in mid-air for a moment as the head end disappeared. Then the galvanized sheeting twanged and for a moment there was nothing.

Somewhere back towards the houses something yelped and the dogs started up. The canal made its small gulping sounds. And I was there alone. An accessory. Breaking and entering. *Me. I don't do things like this*, I thought. The rusty hatch was the entry to another world, one where *people like us* don't go. I could still make it home if I ran now. Mum need never know.

Sly reappeared. "Thanks," she said, and reached an arm

down. "You're a mate. Toss me the torch. Now *you* ..."

Up to the ledge was OK, but once I reached the hatch I squeezed and squirmed and – it must be the extra knees and elbows – stuck. There I was with my face in the brickwork. Sly was bending the corrugated iron back for all she was worth, till I could feel stuff flaking in my hair. I grabbed for my glasses as they slid off and I shut my eyes. Then the galvanized sheet gave an inch more; I was through.

It was dark. Sly hadn't waited. She had dropped down inside with the torch. You could hear it was empty and huge. The odd thing was: outside everything felt so close, even dogs barking half a mile away. In here felt like wide open spaces. You could fit the city in this place and still have room for more. The torch flickered on. "That's better. Hey ..."

It could have been a cave, except that everything was square. Square pillars supported the ceiling, spaced out at square intervals, back and back as far as I could see. It was like a forest, all square trunks with no leaves. The shadows of them criss-crossed as Sly moved. She splashed the beam around, getting bolder as we realized that we had it to ourselves.

In one corner we found a lift shaft in a wire cage. The folding gate was shut, held in place by the steel claw of a safety catch. The lift was up above; two cables looped down like snakes. I fingered the control switch. Sly shook her head hard. She gestured: *up*. "What's that?"

"Wind?" It wasn't a sound, not even a movement, just

... you know that feeling when you *know* that something's there. Something alive.

"You can go back if you like." Sly had found a door through to a stairwell that led up and down. Just for a moment I felt like one of those cartoons where the image splits: two figures walk out of the space where there was only one. Half of me said *OK then* and set off home in a hurry. The other half looked up the shadowy stairs and said "No way."

I could feel the blood buzzing in my skin. I've had that thrill in films – specially the horror ones, the ones that worry Mum – but this was it for real. As we set foot on those stairs I thought of all the books where Something comes in from the night, into the lighted house, in through the window somebody left open. But the Thing in the dark was me.

The next floor was no different from the first. The third one was the same. On the stairs after that, Sly clicked the torch off. We felt one step at a time. Then we noticed we could see, just a little. From the crack of the door came a very faint glow.

Sly was absolutely still. In profile, all her worst points showed up: flat nose, big chin, narrow eyes and roughed-up skin. Her face was like a mask in a museum, from some other place or time. Some Aztec priestess might have worn it.

"It's OK," she said. "No-one there."

The first thought I had was that we'd stumbled into some maniac jumble sale, or a storeroom where every joke shop in the country sent their unsold novelties. There was a dining table that sagged and wobbled when I touched it –

made of rubber. Balanced on it was a wooden ball. The thing I stubbed my toe on seemed to be a glass brick. When I bent to look, I found a beer mug made of stone.

The light came from the far end of a long aisle, through a door that hung ajar. It picked its way among the junk as carefully as we did, lifting out a lamp stand in the shape of an ostrich, or a top hat with horns, or a cuddly teddy bear with claws and teeth. Through the door, on the other hand, I could see a chair, a lamp, a mug, a kitchen sink, all the ordinary things that in this madhouse looked insanely strange.

Sly was still nosing through the jumble. Suddenly she swore, hoarsely. "Look at this."

12.

I tiptoed over to where Sly was kneeling. In the quiet warehouse, every sound I made ran off into the dark in little echoes. Worse, as the echoes faded, there were restless noises from the jumble all around. But the lit room at the far end of the aisle seemed empty.

She knelt by what looked like a coffee table, except for the way it rippled when she shone the flashlight in. In the shallow water there were splodges like the coral stuff in rock pools on the beach. More regular, though. As the surface settled I could see they were light and dark squares. There was a chess board in there and, crawling on it, little pawns and bishops and knights that were the shells of whelks. Easily done, you'll say – except that they seemed to know their moves. The bishop-whelks went only diagonally, rook straight and the knights in wonky zig-zags to and fro.

She flashed the torch at the next tank. Small white mushrooms, that's all. Then as we watched one started to put out small rubbery feelers, like a snail. I jogged the tank. The feelers all pulled back together in a blink. But it was the next tank made me really queasy.

"Sly," I whispered. "Are these plants or what?" They were, surely: Venus fly-traps with jaws open for a meal. Except they were walking about on jointed insect legs. "Are *they*? Are *these*?" she said. "I've got a spider plant with real spiders. Is this all some kind of joke?"

"Least we were wrong about the vivisection."

"Whatever all this is, it's pretty sick. Look out ... "
Crack. Too late: my foot had caught it. Sly's torch picked it out: a china dog, like old ladies have by the fires, only a hundred times more lifelike. Its head broke off and rolled away. As I ducked out of sight, the Chinese vase beside me growled.

We waited for alarms, for voices, something. Nothing. Through the door, the lamp at the kitchen sink burned on. Behind me in the dark, something in a cage creaked hopefully. I didn't want to know what it might be.

Sly's voice was firmer now. "All harmless fun, then, is it? Come and look at these rats."

I winced. They were scaly all over, as if their whole body surface was one tail. The next exhibit was a tank of furry fish. "That's it," said Sly. "Whoever did this, I'll kill them."

"Hold it," I whispered. "Let me think ... " I had a feeling, somehow, all this almost made sense. There was a pattern to it all, if I could make it out. Sly was striding towards the doorway. "Wait!" I said. "They're pick 'n' mixed ... " But she wasn't listening. She had reached the door.

We stood together looking in at what could have been the kitchen of a grotty bedsit. Someone was holed up in here, all right, and not living in style. There was a can of ravioli open by the single Calor gas ring, and a spoon in it, and a whistling kettle on its side with the bottom burned out. There were unwashed coffee cups of several ages, judging by the mould.

"We've seen enough," I said. "Let's get out of here."

Sly shook her head. "There's more," she said. "I just know it. There's worse." She was looking at the other door. It was steel, with a handle like the wheel of a sailing ship. The whole thing was inside a stout steel cage. "That's it," said Sly and stepped into the room.

There was something in the air – weird, queasy; it felt much more than simply fear. If it had been a sound it would have been like monks chanting through their noses in a cave on a Tibetan mountain. Or the slight hum and crackle of high-tension cables, and the feeling you get when you're standing beneath them, pressure building in your head. It took Sly an age to cross that room. I had hours, it seemed, to notice all the little details in the clutter, like the hand-printed poster with a clown's face and a flower wilting in his hat. *MISTER MULTIPLEX*, it said. *CHILDREN'S PARTIES ARE MY SPECIALITY*. It looked faded, smudged and sad.

Sly hauled the bolt of the cage and pushed the gate ajar for me. She manhandled the wheel of the strongroom – it squealed but Sly didn't care, she was strong, she was angry and she heaved the door open with all her weight.

There was a moment's silence as we stared into the dark. Then with a chattering howl something bowled Sly backwards into me. As we fell in a heap, it was up on its hind legs and over us in one bound. Then there was only an animal smell that hung in the air behind it. From the cages and junk out in the hall came a flurry of whistles and snarls. From inside the strongroom came a feeble human groan.

1 3 .

Something stirred on the floor. It groaned again: "Oh no..."

Sly was on her feet. I was still wondering which way was up, but she was ready for action. "Nobody move," she said, just like in the films. "I've got a knife."

It moaned again. "What have you done?"

Sly faltered. I knew what she'd expected: some butcher's slab laboratory, with experiments in progress. Whatever we'd found wasn't that. I was feeling for a light. As I clicked it on, the man on the floor hid his face in his hands. A shabby grey cardigan sagged around him.

"What've *we* done?" Sly said. "We're asking the questions. What's going on?"

"Whatever you think," the man said through his fingers, "... you're wrong."

"Who *are* you, anyway?" Sly snarled. "You the night-watchman or something? Where are the others?" As the man shook his head, the few strands of hair plastered across the top fell back; a bald patch glistened in the half-light. Sly stood above him. "Look at me."

The head came up slowly. I hardly dared watch as the hands slid aside. But nothing in this hall of monstrous things prepared me for the shock of that face. It was the face of a completely ordinary middle-aged man. On second thoughts, not quite ordinary. I'd seen him before – scuttling out of the door of Skinner's shop.

"Where did it go?" he said. "Got to find it. If I don't, God knows ... " He trailed off. "Did you see?"

"See? It hit us."

He nodded and sighed. "Tell me: what was it like?"

"You're asking *us*?" said Sly. "What *is* this?" She stepped towards him, and he flinched.

"Let me explain. Give me a moment, got to catch my breath." He sat there, crumpled from the waist down like a big ventriloquist's dummy. He looked with big eyes, first at Sly, then me. "I need a stiff drink. Be a good man; get the bottle, will you? In the cupboard by the sink."

There was a purple bottle – *Methylated Spirit BP* – and a brownish one of whiskey (not much left). Also a black one, hand-lettered *Oil of Mummia*. The whiskey seemed the safest bet to me. There was a cloudy toothmug on the sink.

"You're lying," I heard Sly snarl as I went back in. "There's got to be someone else. Scientists, somebody ... "

"Good man," he said again, as I put the toothmug in his hands. "Good man." He downed it and shuddered. He looked at Sly. "That's where you're wrong. Oh so wrong. If *only* there was somebody. The truth is: *there's nobody but me* ... and now you're here. It's almost a relief."

"That thing," I said. "What *was* it?"

"Believe me: *I don't know*. I can work it out, roughly." The strongroom was practically empty. There was just a hard chair, fallen backwards, and a couple of large wooden boxes. One of them gaped open, as if it had been wrenched apart. He lifted the lid of the other one cautiously, and peered in. "Oh no," he said again. "That isn't what I meant. No, that's not it at all."

There was a feeble scuffling. "Look," he said. "Have a good look. Isn't that pathetic?"

The little creature cringed in the corner of its box. It had large black eyes that looked as if they were on the point of tears. Suddenly it skipped into the centre of the box as if it was a stage and went into an embarrassing routine of fawning, begging, rolling over on its back for its tummy to be tickled and quivering its stringy tail. When nobody patted it, it turned down the corners of its monkeyish mouth, sagged on its haunches and whined.

It caught sight of Sly. The big moist eyes went twice their usual size; its forehead wrinkled with the effort. It was out of the box and scrabbling at her ankles with small yearning sounds.

"Get off!" Sly shrank back, but it clung on, deep in love. "Yerrch, what is it?"

"Take a good look," sighed the man. "This little fellow here is bad news, very very bad."

"He looks harmless enough to me."

"Precisely. Whatever this one's like, the other one will be the opposite."

1 4 .

I looked at the creature in the box, and I tried to imagine *the opposite*. The opposite of small. The opposite of tame. The opposite of friendly. The opposite of harmless. I stopped trying to imagine, quickly.

"And it's *your* fault!" The crumpled man had clenched a fist; he banged the floor. Then, as if worn out, he sank back.

"Us?" I said. Sly just stared.

"You, my young friends. You burst in at the critical moment. The process was nearly completed. It was the instant when everything hangs in the balance. And then, *then* of all times, you had to burst in! You ... " He poked a finger at us each in turn. "You are responsible for making it ... whatever it is.

"Help me up," he said suddenly. "With any luck it won't have got too far." We all looked at the door. I thought of those dark empty halls out there, and *something* in them, something I didn't have a name for. With any luck it would have got a long, long way away.

Sly squared her jaw. "I don't care what it is. If it's an animal, it should be free." Every time she spoke, the little tail-wagging thing began to blink and quiver. It was making it difficult for her to get properly angry.

"Sly," I said. "Shouldn't we let him explain?"

"Thank you." He settled back. By some sleight of hand he had refilled the toothmug without me noticing. "Funny," he said. "I've dreamed of this – the revelation, as it were. I imagined scientists. The Nobel Prize committee, maybe. But it's you. Two kids.''

"Get on with it," said Sly. "This had better be good.''

"The creature you have just, er, *liberated* . . . '' He paused and squinted at the other one, which was volunteering to be Sly's new slippers, ''. . . will be very agile. Long arms. Good eyes. Considerable intelligence. Plus . . . '' He glanced at us. "Aggressive instincts and sharp teeth.''

Sly's new pet whimpered.

He went on. "Imagine a dog, an Alsatian . . . yes? As fierce as that. And imagine an ape, not quite human but nearly, a gibbon . . . that intelligent.'' He held up his hands. "It wasn't meant to be like *that*. It plexed all wrong.'' His eyes flashed. "It was working – I could handle it, I *know*. Then . . . you burst in!''

"Plexed?'' I said, feebly.

"When I was a young man . . . no, don't interrupt!'' He fixed us with his eyes. "If you don't listen now you'll never understand a thing. Where was I? Yes, when I was young . . . I had dreams. The stage. I knew what I was born to be . . . '' He was looking straight at us but his eyes were focussed far away. "An *actor*. I could have played Hamlet, given chance.'' He shrugged. "I got some parts in pantomime. I believe my Abanazer went down rather well in Stockport. Ah, well . . . '' Somewhere deep in the building came the whispered echo of the echo of a crash. Our host didn't blink. "The years went by. You won't know the feeling, not yet, but you will . . . I did seasons in seaside towns you've never heard of, months on end in boarding houses, writing postcards home until . . . My wife, well, you know how it is, I can't blame her. Then it was boarding houses all the time. When the pantomime came off there were the children's parties – at least the little beasts get *born* all year round. That's where I learned the conjuring routine."

The poster on the wall looked down on us. *MISTER MULTIPLEX.* "Conjuring?" I said. "Is that what it is, all this?"

"No, I was a useless conjuror. Even little ones could spot the tricks. I tried to make a joke of it, but they know when you're down, the monsters. There was a day, a dreadful day, when they started throwing things. Cream cakes, jellies, squashed bananas, anything they could lay their paws on. And the parents laughed. What could I do? Please don't smile. I wanted to die.

"I was surrounded. It was all I could do to shield my face. I picked up a poster in one hand, yes, like that one there. My other hand was up, like this, just in time. Someone had let off one of those balloons, you know, that make rather gross noises." He dared us to laugh. "There it was wriggling in my hand, revolting, like something alive. Suddenly ... " He shuddered. "Suddenly it happened. Both things ... *changed.*"

He reached for the desk and pulled a drawer open. I couldn't help remembering how Dad used to tease me at the seaside, feeling into rockpools and pulling out something really horrid. Mister Multiplex pulled out a mask ... no, it was actually a rubbery blubbery face, a sick shade of green.

"I tore the poster up later," he said. "It *would* make that disgusting noise. But this ... " A smile perched on his lips a moment. "It cleared the room in no time. It went off zooming round the room, like those balloons do, as if it was chasing the little horrors. When it caught up with one it came right up close like *this*!" He thrust the flabby thing towards us. Then he tossed it in the drawer. "And that was the first plex."

"*Plex*?" I said. "Is that a real word?"

"Can you think of a better one?"

"I mean, what's it *really* called?"

"My dear boy, how can it be called anything? It had never been done before." He looked at us both sharply. "Do you believe me?" he said. "If you don't, no-one ever will."

15.

Let's get this straight: this isn't some mad scientist we're talking about. Not some horror-film psycho. He looked like the kind of uncle you only invite once a year. He looked like a bore.

"Who are you?" said Sly. "What's your *real* name."

"*Mister Multiplex* is real enough for me. You might drop the *Mister*, if we are to be friends."

"Not sure about that," she said then, after a pause: "I'm Sly. He's Todd. He's good. I'm not."

"Yes, so I see. Where was I?"

There was this bedsit he lived in. I could see it as he spoke: 40-watt bulb on the stairs, that always went off when you were halfway up. I could smell the stale coffee and mould. That's where he used to practise, on his own. Sometimes, late at night, when he was just about to give up, it would work.

"How?" I said. "What do you *do*?"

"I don't know. You've got to be sort of . . . empty. Then the power comes." He shrugged. "I tried it in the Plume of Feathers. Simple things – a glove and a shoe, plex them, you get a slipper-sock with toes, you get a boxing glove. Hey presto. People bought me drinks. That's when I started thinking of . . . the possibilities . . . What I didn't think of was the *other side*."

"What other side? The other side of what?"

"Of . . . whatever you want. Don't you see: that's how it works? Take two things, choose what you want from each, mix them. The best of both worlds! Isn't that what we all want?" He looked straight at us.

"Pick 'n' mix," I said. "You mean you could . . . *plex* two people and . . . " I glanced at Sly. ". . . get someone with good eyesight *and* good spelling, and . . . "

"Not people," he said quickly. "Things, yes. *Life* is something different."

"Wait a mo!" This was Sly. "Those things out there . . . *that's life*, isn't it?"

He let his face droop. "Try to understand," he said. "Try to imagine. You're nothing. Useless. All your life, you've known deep down: you've got no talent. Other people have; you haven't. And it gets worse, till one day . . ." He shrugged. "Despair. Simple as that. And then . . . right out of the blue, you've got this gift. Magic. People's faces light up. They want more!"

"Huh," said Sly. "Some party trick."

"A trick? Sometimes I wish it *was*. Oh, I've done what all magicians do – I've used props. Oil of Mummia sounds rather good. Things like that help hide the times it doesn't work . . . which it didn't, a lot of the time. So I'd start to get desperate, just about to give up, and then . . . it did!"

He looked at me. "The worst part is: you need it more and more. It's like a drug. You start imagining that *one step more*. One more rung up the ladder. Plants at first, then simple animals – insects, snails, where's the harm in that? Maybe a small reptile . . . "

His face was flushed. He looked as if he might have some

sort of attack. "You can't stop. It gets harder, of course. The more complex the organism, the more energy it takes. Look at me now!" He was still limp and trembling from the effort of it. "And the more it can go wrong ... "

"Why can't you stop? Give it up. Go back to ..."

"Back to what?" he broke in. "There's nothing to go back to. No home, no family, no friends. But I've got *this*." He waved a hand towards the darkened halls. "My little empire. My world. I could make anything." From somewhere out there came a muffled thud.

"The gog," I said.

"The what?" said Sly.

"Dog/gibbon." I heard myself giggle. Stupid. If only this was the Association for Unthinkable Animals. If only I was making all this up. "This one's a dibbon. And *the other side* ... a gog."

The best of both worlds. Makes sense. What's left over's got to be the worst. Neat bit of thinking, that ... except when the worst of both worlds is a thing with claws and teeth, and it's in the darkness out there, waiting.

"I just needed a guard dog," he said. "Only better: something fierce but tame, intelligent, faithful. I could have done it, but for you." He gave us a desperate look. "The things were starting to escape."

"The pterodactyl!" I said. "That was ... *plexed*?"

"Crocodile – cayman, actually – and bat." It could have been a recipe: *Half a pound of* ... "It's not illegal," he said quickly. "Not protected species."

Sly was digging the toe of her boot in the floor. "And the

gibbon? That's an ape. You can't import that." She knew her stuff, did Sly, give her that.

"You're right," he said. "Of course, you're right. It's Skinner, you see. He keeps egging me on. *Got a nice one for you this time, Mister M. Ever thought of a wallaby? A lemur?* You see what I mean?"

"Nice little earner," Sly said bitterly. "*Exotic pets!*"

"No! I'd never let *him* have a plexing. I keep them safe with me."

Another thump out in the dark. Then a crash. Caged things chittered and whined. "The catwalk door," he said. "It's out."

"And you're going to get it back!" Sly had him by the collar.

"Young lady . . . To capture *that*, single-handed . . ."

"Not single-handed." She looked at me. "We'll help."

"Uh, Sly," I said. "I thought you said animals ought to be free."

"Of course they ought to . . . in their natural habitat. But that thing hasn't got a habitat. It doesn't belong anywhere. It never will. We've got to rescue it and," she turned on Multiplex, "we've got to make him *change it back*."

1 6 .

You never see how strange things are – not normally, I mean. Maybe that's what *normal* is: not noticing. Not noticing how every terraced house is like a face screwed up sideways, sort of saying: *really! Well I never!* Normal means not noticing that houses are basically boxes to store people in for the night. All those people, laid out in their nighties and their pink pyjamas, snoring, breathing, dreaming their own weird dreams.

A cat came towards me, straight down the pavement. It was still on its night-beat; it expected me to get out of its way. It nosed around a bin. It was Thursday. All the bins were out: big black trundle-bins on wheels. They looked fat and satisfied, as if they were the real inhabitants of the place. The people in the houses were just there to feed them. A night without sleep makes you think stuff like that.

The gog. It was out there somewhere, that creature with no proper name and no proper place to be. "No natural habitat," Sly had said. I disagreed. This place had always been its habitat, all these years, just waiting for the creature to appear.

There was a long squeal from the far end of the street. The dustcart was up and about. Its orange light flashed on the curtained windows. Three or four men in orange waist-coats were trudging ahead of it, manhandling bins. Then I was outside my very own stripped and varnished door. It opened, just like that. The Step came out. I should have known. It was his job to put out the rubbish, Wednesday evenings; regular as clockwork he forgot. He had a white sack from the swing-bin in the kitchen in his arms. We faced each other over it. He was more surprised than me.

"Ssssh," I said. "I can explain."

There were two options: honesty (and who in their right mind would believe me?), or bluff. I'd known that from the moment Sly and I had slipped out of the warehouse into the almost-light of dawn and she was off, just a glance over her shoulder: "Be there, OK?" I had to lie my way through this bit on my own.

"Sleepwalking," I said.

The Step stood with his hand on the doorknob. Then he pulled the door gently shut. He leaned close. The bin bag smelt of last night's fish.

"When I came to, I was outside in the street."

He frowned. He was trying to believe me but finding it hard. "You're dressed."

"Sleepwalkers do that. They get dressed, brush their teeth, all the normal things, only they don't remember." I'd read a book from the library; I knew. He didn't look convinced. "Sometimes it's stress," I said. It was a desperate throw. "Kids often get it. When they've got problems at home."

He let the doorknob go. "Todd," he said. "Todd, if there's anything you need to talk about ... I know it isn't easy. I've never pretended I could be a father to you, but ... I'd like to think you could talk to me. Like a friend."

"Thanks," I said. "I'd really like to. Some time when we're on our own."

He nodded. This was a conspiracy.

"Help me slip back upstairs," I said. "Mum needn't know." He looked worried again. "I mean, let's not worry her," I said.

It was half an hour later she knocked on my door. It was no problem sounding sleepy. "Wanna lie in."

"I don't like it." Her voice was muffled. "All this sleeping in the daytime. You should get out more." It was a normal day again. I flopped out on the bed and fell asleep.

★   ★   ★

"There it goes!"

"My God, what IS it?"

"It's the monster."

"It's cornered. Let's get it."

"Keep back. Send for the police."

There is a crunch of tyres. Blue lights are flashing through the girders of the iron bridge. Just say the word, and they appear: that's the way it is with dreams.

The beast flinches. It has pin-drop hearing; the crowd's whisper bothers it like flies. It can pick up the raspy staccato of the walkie-talkies in the panda cars. "Yes, marksmen, quick . . . we're not taking any chances."

There's a quiver in the air, like background music. I can feel my heart speeding now: fight-or-flight. I hold my breath. I don't know if I want to cheer, or cry.

A smack of white light, nothing like daylight, hits the warehouse wall, as the floodlights come on. There are no greys; everything is black or white. On the criss-cross girders of the gasholder, there is one shape, only one, that isn't straight or square. It clings, very still. The cries of its pursuers close in: there! there! kik! kik! geddim! hiss hiss ... haaa!

They're like animal cries; I know what they mean, though I can't grasp the words. I know what they want. They want to kill. I feel my hair bristling all over me, my long fine hair, and I shield my sensitive eyes from the glare of twenty full moons that have suddenly risen all at once. There is the snick of something metal, dangerous ...

I turn and leap. Ten feet away, the next girder offers itself to my strong and hairy hand, as easy as walking upstairs. Something pings and whistles way above. They're hopelessly slow, the clumsy things that want to kill me. My senses are sparking with danger, and the shadows guard me: they are my friends. There's a second of danger as I wobble on a wire fence, then I'm over, running double-power, arms and legs. Now I squat on a heap in a scrapyard, in a little cave of wrecked cars. I listen: nothing. They've lost me. Now I'm on my own.

After a while I move on. Something rises up inside me, starting in my gut. I've got to eat. Now my eyes and ears are tuned again, for any live thing's movement. What was that? A rat? A cat?

I flex my powerful claws. They feel good, though a voice in the back of my head is saying NO! NO! louder and louder. It's hauling me up, up and out of the dream, saying HORRIBLE, HORRIBLE, just as my mouth fills with saliva and I feel my strong teeth sinking into firm, warm, living meat.

★   ★   ★

I opened my eyes and Mum was standing by the bed. Seems I'd been making noises in my sleep. "I didn't know *what* it was," she said. "Serves you right for sleeping in the day."

1 7 .

There was nothing on gibbons in the library, except a couple of pictures in the children's section. I needed facts. The assistant gave me a blank look. "Try the *Encyclopaedia Britannica*, if you like," she said. "You've got three minutes. We're entitled to our lunch hour too." Then I was back in the High Street and I knew where I had to go.

I peered through the grimy barred windows of the shop. A great frilled iguana stared back. It was no contest. It could have given me a million-year handicap and still outstared me. I couldn't see Skinner. I took a deep breath and went in.

The door spring gave a little *ping*! and a hundred cages came alive with scuffles and the scrabbling of little claws. The shop was a cave lined with tanks and cages, most of them with little heat-lamps that sent an orangish glow into the gloom. In the farthest corner, at a counter, Skinner had a customer. I could tell at a glance she wouldn't be there long.

Skinner leaned back on his stool. "Nothing I can do about that," he said. "It left the shop in good condition. Healthy bird." I couldn't make out what the woman was saying; she kept on breaking down in sobs. Skinner watched her coolly. "What did you expect to feed it on?" he said at last.

"Nuts, seeds of course ... maybe a little fruit," she gulped. "For a treat. That's what Coriander's parrot book said."

"Your Kea," Skinner sighed, "is a carnivore. Well known fact in New Zealand. Sheep farmers hate them. Kill the lambs to eat their kidneys, see." When the new storm of sobbing subsided he added, "Shame about your Pekinese."

I didn't turn round, not even when the door *pinged* again, and then shut with a rattling slam. Things scuffled a little, then the shop was quiet, all but a little creaking sound. From the corner of my eye I could see Skinner sitting at the counter, doing finger-strengthening exercises with a little metal spring thing. He wasn't looking at me, but he was watching me, I could tell.

I don't know much about hunting, but my instincts told me: this is what it's like to be the prey. I moved from cage to cage slowly, though the hairs of my scalp were prickling and my heartbeat was going wild. In the latest cage a scorpion crouched, tail at the ready, perched on its stone as peaceful as a trap about to spring. I gave the glass a casual tap. It tensed and started walking backwards stiffly, bumping into things.

"Straight from Egypt, that one." Skinner was right behind me. I hadn't even heard him get up. He was a hunter, all right. His voice was surprisingly soft, like a cat's paw, toying with a mouse. "Got a contact there knows this special cave. So many scorpions, he scoops them up with a shovel. What can I do for you, kid? You don't look like a goldfish man to me ... "

"Oh, nothing. I mean ... " This was happening too fast. I should have come in with my lines prepared. "I mean, they're fantastic, all these things. From all over the world."

"Like I said, I've got contacts."

Keep talking, Todd. "Have you been there, all those places?"

"Most of them. South East Asia specially, and Africa." There was something in his voice. Something like pleasure.

"On holiday?"

"More in the line of business."

"Cor, wish I had a job like that."

He laughed. It didn't sound funny. "Do you? Places like Angola? Or Biafra? Vietnam?"

"You mean ... in the army."

"One army or another. You learn a lot that way. Animals are easy, after that."

"You mean they don't shoot back." I bit my tongue. Skinner went very taut. "I mean ... I mean, you've got brains as well as brawn."

He looked at me. "You've got a nerve, kid." Then he grinned. "I like that. You're not such a weed as you look. Still," he added. "Watch your lip."

There was an awkward pause. "Another thing," I said. "School project ... got to find out everything we can about ... about apes. Well, gibbons, really ... "

He nodded very slowly. Apart from that, the scorpion could not have been more still.

18.

"You *told* him? Skinner!" Sly twined her fingers in the wire fence; I could see her knuckles going white.

"No! Not a thing." Above us, the warehouses waited. "I think he suspected something, though."

"What did he say?"

"Nothing, nothing much. I think it was when, let me see, yes, when I asked him ... "

"Go on."

"... could they live in the wild, in this country. He laughed and said they'd have a heck of a long way to walk from Borneo. And I said: what if one escaped from a zoo? He said: no zoo round here, the question don't arise. And then he came up really close and said: Son, if you ever saw an animal like that round here, you'd need an expert. Don't try and do nothing yourself, he said. And worst of all don't call the cops, they don't know what to do, you see. Needs *very* careful handling, he said. If you see anything like that round here, he said, you just call me, you understand? But I didn't tell him anything."

"Like heck you didn't," said Sly. "For a little Einstein you can be really dim."

"He's a businessman," I said. "If this got out, he'd be in trouble."

"It *has* got out!"

"The news, I mean."

"Yes, and I mean *it*, the gog, the thing. It's an animal."

She was quivering. "Not a proper one but it's alive. It feels pain, the same as you and me."

"I learned something," I said. She glowered. "Gibbons aren't nocturnal. Neither are dogs. So we can be pretty sure *it's* not."

"So?" Sly looked around, warily. It was awake, then, somewhere, now.

"And gibbons and dogs are both social animals. They live in packs or families."

"So?" she said again.

"So ... I don't know. I guess it must be lonely, just the one of it."

Then neither of us could think of anything to say. I looked over our skyline: beyond the warehouses, the girders of the gasholder were painted grey, to match the sky, I guess. I could just see the ragged, rusty edge of the dump in the car-crusher's yard.

"Come on," said Sly. "Let's do something. Anything. There are bound to be tracks, or ... or something."

A feeling came over me – one I didn't like at all. "You know the scrapyard. Yes? Don't ask me why, but I think we might find something there."

"What, the gog?"

"I hope not," I said.

From the footbridge we could see that there was no-one in the yard. There never was, as far as I could see, though the heap of wrecked cars seemed to grow week by week, by itself. We climbed the gate and tiptoed in among the piles.

The feeling of the dream was round me, almost like a smell. Getting stronger, this way, round that corner, there . . .

Up between a charred Cortina and a concertina'd Beetle was a hollow, a scrap-metal cave. I nodded at it. "After you?" Neither of us moved.

"I think he said gibbons are vegetarian," I said, hopefully.

"You mean it's fifty-fifty?" Sly picked up a stone and tossed it neatly into the opening, ducking back round a corner as she did. We waited. Nothing. No-one at home.

When we felt sure enough we wouldn't find anything, we clambered up. Carefully. There were edges of torn metal everywhere that could tear us sure as claws. Then we climbed back down. "Well?" said Sly when we got there. "What now?" Then she turned very pale.

I looked where she was looking. At first I didn't recognize the object as a cat's head. It was ripped quite neatly off. The gog hadn't fancied that bit, but had made a good job of the rest. There was the tail just by my foot, and the odd crunched bone, the odd gobbet of fur. Besides that, just the blood, soaking into the concrete. I suspected – no, I somehow knew – our gog would have lapped up most of that as well.

19.

"Ta-ra!" the Step said. "Rissoles! Totally veggie." We were doing a family mealtime and the Step was trying hard. He took a mouthful. "Oh. Could do with a bit of a sauce. Still, we learn." They tasted like mouthfuls of old exercise book to me.

There was a tactful silence. When Mum's tactfully silent, you know there's something really wrong.

"Todd ... " she said. She eased her plate aside.

"Todd ... " The door bell rang.

"I'll go," said the Step. Mum took a slow breath and started again.

Clunk, the front door jerked open and the knocker rattled. (It always sticks, however many times he sands it down.) My veggie rissole fell off my fork. The voice at the door was Mister Multiplex.

The Step looked back in. "Sorry ... Todd, a man from the library, for you."

"From the library?" Mum said. "Why?"

The Step gave that awkward little shrug of his. "How should I know?"

"I'll sort it out," Mum said.

I ducked between them and into the hall, pushing the door shut behind me. Multiplex was framed in the doorway, large as life. This was it. Whatever was going to happen, it had started happening *now*.

He had on a shabby old jacket with a bit of sheepskin

round the collar, and a little tartan scarf like Rupert Bear. His hair had been brushed across the bald patch, and was coming adrift again. He wore a rather desperate little smile. Nothing definitely odd. But if Einstein's Cheetah had just screeched to a halt on the doorstep, panting, it couldn't have seemed more strange.

"Forgive the intrusion," he said in nothing like his normal voice, "... into the, er, happy home, but ... " His eyes fixed mine. They opened wide and did not blink. I started to see how, as an actor, he must have been a dreadful ham.

"I'm from the library." He aimed the words over my shoulder, back down the hall. "About your *reservation* ... " A meaningful pause. "The book on, er ... *animals*. You recall?"

"Oh, yes ... " I fumbled. "Is it *in*?"

"Alas, no. It is *out at the moment* but ... we *know where it might be*." He gave a slow stage-nod.

"So do I," I whispered.

"Oh," he said. Another glance behind me, then he came up near. "I can't do it without you. You said you'd help. You will, won't you?" What could I do? I nodded. "At dusk," he whispered. "It must be at dusk."

"Why dusk? Won't it be sleeping?"

"If there's any gibbon in it – and there is – we've got a fifty-fifty chance that it might just sing."

I shuddered. The thought of what it might mean, for *that* to *sing*.

Back in the breakfast room (the Step had *knocked it through* so the smell of burnt toast could drift right through the house) I ate up my horrible rissoles like a good boy. Mum was looking at me but I didn't meet her eye. Then I yawned the best yawn I could do. "I think I'll put my light out early," I said. Mum's always telling me to put my light out early; she could hardly say no. "Goodnight," I said. I went up to my room and closed the door hard so they could hear. Then I tiptoed back downstairs, hooked my anorak off the peg and pulled the sticky door shut behind me, very carefully indeed.

It was getting dark early for August. The clouds were down on the warehouse roofs. For a moment I prayed: yes, let it rain. But it didn't. Rain did not stop play.

The Zetland Street Flats may well have been state-of-the-art accommodation once, a hundred years ago. Maybe the men who built the warehouses slapped them up with the left-over bricks. The numbers for number 15 had come off the door – I could see the screw-holes. There were two bare wires where the bell had been. If I touched them together it might ring, but this wasn't the time or the place, somehow, for clever stuff. I knocked at the door.

The toddler who opened it stared. "I . . . I wanted Sl . . . Sally-Ann," I stumbled. The kid turned and called: "Sal . . . Someone for you."

The hallway jiggled with a faint blue glow. Inside, a television bickered with itself in Australian. Then Sly was pushing through towards me. "Who's he, Sal?" One or two of the little ones came pushing after.

"It's her boyfriend, it's her boyfriend." Giggle. A back-handed slap. "Ma! Sal hit me!"

Sly cast one look back, then pushed me backwards onto the landing. "Don't mind them," she muttered. "Is it on?" I nodded. "Great," she said, and grinned. "Come on, partner. We've got work to do."

20.

Sly thumped on the green steel door. It echoed deep inside. Above our heads the catwalk creaked but I could only just make out its outline. Night was coming early. Sly thumped again.

"Who is it?" Multiplex's voice was muffled.

"Us."

"Just you?"

"Yes."

There was a pause, then the door slid sideways, just a crack. He looked like a small wary animal peeping out of its hole. "You came," he said. "Thank you! No-one else knows, do they?"

Sly looked hard at me. "Tell him."

Mister Multiplex's face sagged. "Oh, no. I trusted you. Who knows? Your mother and father? They seemed . . . less than sympathetic."

"Not them." I squirmed. "The pet man, Skinner . . . he might have guessed something."

"Give me patience!" Multiplex lifted both hands to the sky. Then he dropped them and shrugged, as if to say: *I'm used to it, it happens all the time.* "Well," he said. "That explains it. He was round here earlier, asking questions. Nothing specific, but . . . Ah, well. Can't be helped. We'll just have to find it before he can."

There was a sudden scuffling round his knees, all breathy whimpers. The little dibbon-thing slipped out of his grasp and launched itself at Sly. "Oh, no, not *that*," she said.

"Sorry, it's been pining. Terribly affectionate. Probably they bond for life." Sly had her Doc Marten raised, but she stopped in mid-swing. "Hold on, I've had an idea. The other thing, when we find it . . . how are we going to get close to it? Hold out a bone and say: here, nice doggie?" Both of us looked at Multiplex. Again, that shrug. It would have been too much to hope that he might just have a *plan*.

"OK," said Sly. "This one here, if it was with us . . . don't you think the what d'you call it, gog, may be missing its other half, too?"

She was brilliant, was Sly. The attraction of opposites . . . why couldn't I have thought of something so simple and so right? Multiplex looked at her long and hard, then nodded: "Why not? Why not indeed?"

We assembled the capture-kit together. He had a good-sized net, heavy grade, *very* tough; I didn't know whether to be reassured by this or quite the opposite. There were leather straps with buckles and a muzzle like a medieval instrument of torture. "That big?" I said, faintly. He nodded: yes, that big. He held a hypodermic up to check it in the failing light.

"Sedative," he said. "One shot of this and he'll come peaceful as a lamb." *A lamb with fangs*, I thought, but thought better of saying it. Multiplex was folding the kit into a shopping bag on wheels, the kind of thing old ladies take down to the supermarket. The dibbon chittered with excitement. "Shut up," Sly said. It clapped one hand, like the *Speak No Evil* monkey, across its mouth.

"Not that way." Multiplex waved us inside. "Not *over* the footbridge." He clanged the door behind us. "I'll take you out the back door, as it were."

His torch beam led us down the stairwell, through a basement – totally empty as far as I could see, but then again, who wants to look? In the furthest corner a huge pipe led into, and straight through, the wall. Between it and the ragged brickwork, there was space for even a slack bag of innards like Multiplex to squeeze through. Then we were out in the air, with a strong sniff of canal beneath our feet.

Beneath the footbridge was a narrow plank, a workmen's walkway, maybe, with the pipe on one side and a drop on the other. It wasn't that far down, but it wasn't inviting. In the dark, the water moved like black treacle. If you fell in it would not let go. "Watch the dibbon," he said.

The creature was dancing along the plank with all the confidence of animal instinct. It was wrong. It missed its footing, grabbed at Sly, and hand met paw. She tugged it across. Then we were underground, where the pipe led straight into the canal side. A few yards of squeezing in darkness, then Multiplex stopped to struggle with a little wooden door. When it eased open, we were looking out onto a road. "*Voilà!*" he said. "Hey presto."

"A secret entrance!" I said.

He beamed: "Exactly. Always was a master of concealment and prestidigitation . . ."

Sly gave him a come-off-it look, then slipped through. I slipped after. I was just about to reach up to help the other two down, when Sly hissed: "Back!" Multiplex's face and one arm, clamped around the dibbon, shrank back like a snail in its shell.

"What is it?" I said. I couldn't understand why she didn't answer. She just stared behind my head. Slowly I followed her stare, and turned to face a figure that stepped out of the shadows, grinning, with a gun.

2 1 .

"Magic, eh?" Skinner's teeth gleamed white in the half-light. "Appearing out of nowhere?" He looked closer. "*You!* So there *is* something doing."

"No," I said weakly. "We're just ... hanging out, that's all."

"Oh yeah? Kid like you, *hanging out*? Come off it. Bet your Mummy and Daddy don't know you're here. And who's this?"

"I can answer for myself," snapped Sly. "Never you mind. But I know you. I know what you are."

"Yeah? What?"

"I know about you and your animals ... "

Slowly Skinner grinned. "So-o-o. You're *not* 'just hanging out'. Let's drop the games. We all know why we're here." He glanced up at the warehouse. "It's him, isn't it? He's let it escape, stupid berk. He's let the gibbon out."

I looked at Sly; she looked at me. He knew a lot, did Skinner, but there was still one thing he didn't know. We weren't going to tell him. "Oh, the ... the gibbon," I said. "Yes."

"Well ... " Suddenly his voice was soft and soothing. "So we've got to get it back. Poor thing. It's a hostile environment. The thing'll starve. Look, I know about these things."

Sly was staring at the slim black rifle he was holding.

"Don't worry," he purred. "It fires darts, not bullets. Just to stun it for an hour or two ... Trust me."

Sly said a word I'd never be allowed to say at home. "Watch it, you little punk." Skinner took one swift step towards her. "You get in my way and ... " As he stepped forward Sly shrieked and jumped back; she crouched, she snarled, she seemed to have claws and teeth. And in the moment's hush that followed, a long warbling whimper came from the hatch in the wall. Skinner turned. "Well, well ... you're hiding something up there. You know what that is, don't you?" Sly clamped her jaw shut; so did I. "You could save me a lot of bother," said Skinner. "Do I have to go and drag it out?"

"Don't you dare!" Sly had jumped between him and the wall. "Over my dead body," she said.

Skinner laughed – a laugh in slow motion. "If that's how you want it ... "

"Stop!"

We all looked up. Mister Multiplex's face appeared in the hatchway. "Don't touch her. I can explain." He was struggling out of the narrow entrance, the dibbon clinging to his trousers. Suddenly he missed his footing and fell. He hit the ground with a flat *ooof!* and for a moment lay there motionless. A paw appeared from underneath him, then an arm. The dibbon dragged itself out groggily. It tugged at his arm and whimpered. Mister Multiplex's eyelids fluttered. He looked up.

Skinner was staring at the dibbon. "What the hell is *that?*" He peered closer. "Wait a minute. So-o-o ... he's been playing again. Playing the fool with the laws of nature.

This is one of your weird things, isn't it?" You could hear him thinking. He was getting there. "Ye-e-es. And whatever you're looking for, it's not this. It's the *other side* thing, isn't it? Yeah ... " He looked at the dibbon and nodded slowly. "Now *that* would be worth having, wouldn't it?" He leaned over Multiplex and in one heave jerked him to his feet. "Tell me about it. Your masterpiece!"

"No."

Skinner's arm snaked out; he had me by the wrist; my arm was up behind me and I yelped, I couldn't help it. "Well," he said. "My friend here will talk, won't you? *You* want to be on the *men's* side for a change, don't you? Not with this girl and this old freak."

"Let him go," yelled Sly. "He didn't see it. None of us did."

"Curious," said Skinner. "He knows something, though, I can see it. I think he wants to help his old mate Skinner. We could be a team." He twitched the rifle at them. "You two ... and that thing. I'll see you later. Wait at the van. It's by the footbridge. Move." They stared a moment, then began to back away. "Wait," Skinner said, quite quietly. "Don't even *think* of calling anybody." He yanked my arm up and I yelped again. "Or things could get really messy. Don't try anything."

22.

"Don't get me wrong," said Skinner. We were inside the fence, beneath the sign: WASTE PAPER RECLAMATION PLANT. KEEP OUT. "I want this thing alive. Think what it's worth. It's like catching a Yeti, a Bigfoot, the Loch Ness Monster, only better, because this is *the only one*. Ever. Think what they'd pay for that."

We moved down a strange white canyon in the half-light. Stacked sheaves of shredded paper rose on either side, three or four times our height, like ragged cliffs or icebergs. Every now and then, the whole place riffled in the breeze. It sounded restless. Everything was ready to begin.

Skinner was a big man and all muscle, but he moved without a sound. He kept me in the corner of his eye, within a hand's grab. I was breathless trying to keep up, and it wasn't just the exercise. I didn't want to, but I couldn't help it: I was feeling the excitement of the hunt.

The sky was lower than ever, and heavy with the threat of rain. Every now and then there was a low rumble that might have been a late goods train on the railway bridge, or thunder. Once, an odd rush of wind ripped a strip of paper off the stack and it swooped off above us like a hunting owl. Skinner stopped, crouched, listening. Nothing. He whispered: "Tell me about this creature. Anything."

"I don't know," I said. "Only that it knocked us over. It was big."

"It can't be *that* big. Just a dog and a gibbon ... "

"You saw the other one. That's smaller than either. This one could be bigger, just to balance out. Oh, and it eats meat ... "

Skinner didn't answer. Very soft at first, there was a sound, that rose and rose into a kind of gulping howl, as if a wolf had tried yodelling. We froze. Twice, three times the cry went up and hung in the air. It must have been waiting for an answer – marking its territory or calling a mate. But that would take another of its own kind, and there wasn't one, not in the world, and never would be. By the end of the third cry Skinner had us moving quickly, keeping cover, towards the gasholder that reared behind the paper plant. Suddenly he stopped me. "Look."

I saw it at last. A long way up among the girders, in silhouette against the street-glow in the clouds, there was a lumpy shape. "OK," he said. "So it's big. I'll grant you that." But he was moving on already. "Got to get closer," he whispered. "Got to have a clear shot." There was a corrugated fence between us and the waste ground round the gasholder. At a glance, he'd found the one loose sheet. He bent it back for me.

I was clumsier than him. The corrugated iron whipped back with a click behind me. Skinner swore under his breath, but didn't spare a glance for me. He was looking up, high in the girders, where the shape had moved.

"Damn," he said. "You've scared it. Now it'll climb up for safety and ... Hey ... " He had stiffened. "Good." He grinned. "It's coming down to talk to us."

I could see it dropping in smooth swings from girder to girder. Skinner had the rifle to his shoulder. He was cool,

I'll give him that. He stepped out into the open, just to make sure it had seen him. It had. It was coming faster.

"Look ..." I started.

He snarled: "Shut it, kid." When it was ten metres up, he squeezed the trigger: *phut!* The gog jerked, stopped in its smooth glide down a moment ... then kept on coming.

"It'll slow down," he said. "That stuff's powerful." Then it dropped. There was a dull clang as it hit the lid of the sunken gas tank, out of sight. "There," Skinner said. "Give it a minute, then we pick up the winnings."

A minute? It felt like an hour or two. The night was very quiet. Even the city was holding its breath. Then there was another murmur of thunder, far away. "OK," he said. "Follow me."

I followed his boots up the steel stairs where the first zig-zag of ladder started up the gasholder frame. I could have turned and ran, I suppose, but right then it seemed that next to Skinner was the safest place to be. As we stepped out on the first ledge we looked down towards the wide lid like an emptied swimming pool, where the stunned gog would be lying. Except it wasn't there.

23.

Skinner didn't speak for a while. He was scanning the gasholder like an empty stage. Inch by inch, shadow by shadow. He was listening and frowning and sniffing the air. "Hold this," he said suddenly, tossing the dart gun to me.

"What do I do?" I said. He'd slipped out another gun, more businesslike, an army pistol by the look of it. "You do nothing. If you see a movement, shout."

His face looked different all of a sudden. I thought: for once *he isn't sure*. This wasn't much comfort to me. "You said you'd got it," I said. "You said it was slowing down ..." I felt the words coming faster and faster; I couldn't stop them. "Now it's out there somewhere, isn't it? You said we were hunting it. It's hunting *us!*"

"Shut it!" Skinner gripped my arm. He shook me hard. "Listen to me. We don't panic. We just climb down off of here. Quickly. You first. Go!" I reached the ground. Skinner was there a moment later. That's when, for the second time, we heard the howl. It came from everywhere, all round us. All the girders seemed to ring with it. There was more of a growl in it this time, more of a bark, and it was *loud*. Skinner whipped round this way and that, gun at the ready. He was rattled. "Cool it," he said. "It's a trick of the sound. The echoes ... " We both looked up. The girders hung above us like a metal spider's web. He took me by the sleeve and pushed me. "Make for the fence."

I reached the loose place in the corrugated sheeting first

and pushed straight through. Then he was beside me, squinting back through. "A tactical retreat," he said. He frowned as though he'd seen something, then couldn't be sure. To me, all the shadows seemed to have lives of their own.

"You mean we're running away?"

He jerked me to my feet so hard I thought he was going to hit me, but he just said, "We need some clear ground. Back to the road."

We were back in the waste-paper canyons. On the way, they'd seemed straightforward. Now they branched and zigzagged. The wind seemed to have died down again, and there was a heavy stillness. That's when we heard the sound behind us: first a long creak, then a short sharp crack. Then the rasp of a torn sheet of corrugated iron fencing, tossed aside. A gust of wind rose in the paper mountains with a steady ripping sound.

"Keep calm," said Skinner. "Keep your back to mine. Keep watching. Don't stop moving. Now, slowly ... " Thump. Something burst behind us with a punchbag thud. A large bale hit the ground, just feet away, exploding in a cloud of shredded paper; the wind showered it round us like confetti. I think that's when I dropped the dart gun, but I don't know. We just ran.

Skinner got to the gate first. Now he wasn't waiting for me, but I caught up as he rattled it. It wouldn't give. He raised his gun. The crack stung my eardrums and the padlock flew apart. He wrenched the gate. We didn't stop till we had the road between us and the waste yard, with our backs to a comforting wall.

We didn't move. He crouched, the gun trained on the

gate, eyes flickering this way and that. But nothing bounded out of the shadows. Nothing scaled the fence. You could almost have felt it had all been imagination, and nothing had been there at all.

The thunder was close now – still not loud but all over the sky, as if it was tiptoeing just behind the clouds. A big drop of rain burst on the pavement, and I jumped. Another drop. Another. In a moment it would pour. "What now?" I said.

"We need more equipment. You got a better plan?"

"Can't we just . . . leave it?"

"Leave it? That? You heard it. One night of that and you'll have the *News At Ten* down here. The place'll be crawling."

"So?"

"Publicity. It's bad for business." Skinner came up close. "You just remember that. I've got interests to protect. You say *nothing* about this. Not to anybody. Nothing. Understand?"

There was a squawk. A long shape twanged like elastic out of the waste yard. Skinner swivelled and tensed in one move, taking aim. The crack of the pistol bowled the creature over and it lay still. Skinner moved towards it, cautiously. He bent over it. "Cat!" As he bent, I looked over his head. Up the road, where we'd been, a much larger shadow flickered – one crouch in the road, then a spring. "There!" Skinner's reflexes were quick but in the moment it took for him to look where I was pointing, it was gone, up or into the wall. He didn't hesitate now. "Move it. Back to the van."

24.

Everything was out to get me. The two iron bollards at the end of the footbridge, put there to keep cyclists out, swiped at me as I dodged past. I didn't feel the pain. I was running like I'd never run before, but as I ran my mind was moving faster, overtaking me.

Where had the creature gone? How had it vanished into a brick wall? Of course – the hatch, the pipe, the secret entrance. The way to the warehouse ... or to cut us off. I remembered the plank across the canal – the plank which was right beneath the footbridge which was ... right beneath me now.

The sides of the bridge were criss-cross strips of iron, topped by a rusty handrail. There were square gaps big enough for a hand or a foot to fit through. I didn't look. That's why I didn't see the movement through the girders, not till something curled out, long, more tentacle than arm, but hairy. Slap. As it clamped my ankle I fell full length, hard. Then it began to pull.

I must have yelled, because Skinner turned and started back towards me. I was kicking like mad, but the paw, or the claw, whatever it was, tightened. It was dragging me towards the edge. I twisted round and caught a glimpse, through the lattice-work of iron, of the gog's snout. Of its teeth.

"Brace yourself," yelled Skinner, as I grated up against cold iron. Thinking back, I can see what he meant. If I stayed stiff, it couldn't pull me through. Not that this would stop it trying. Hard to think that clearly, when you're close enough to smell the creature's breath.

It had thought the same thought. Another arm swiped over the handrail and down; it had me by the shoulder. At the same moment Skinner was beside me and for a moment I thought it would be a tug o' war, with me as the rope that would snap. He thrust the pistol past me, right between the girders where I'd seen the thing's face, and he fired.

The force knocked me sideways. Claws ripped through my anorak at the shoulder, scoring through the flesh as well. But I was free. As I rolled away, gasping, there was a sudden eerie stillness on the footbridge. Then a dull splash. Skinner swore.

"I didn't want to have to do that," he said, as if it was my fault. "What a waste." He helped me upright, none too gently, and peeled the ripped anorak off for a look at the arm. "Flesh wound," he said. Then it was business again. "There's still the other creature."

"He'll never let you have it," I said. "Never. He said so." We both looked up to see we had an audience: Mister Multiplex and Sly, at the end of the footbridge, staring, waiting, like he told them, by the van.

In one of those moves so swift and strong you could tell he'd practised it on people, Skinner had my arm up behind my back. "He will," he said, and pushed me forwards. "Go on, whimper," he said. "It'll help." To Multiplex he called: "An exchange. The boy for your monster." No-one moved. "Come on." Skinner rattled my arm, my hurt arm, in its armlock; I gasped. "Human for animal. What're you waiting for?" That's when I heard the Step's voice. It called: "Todd?"

"Into the bushes," Skinner hissed. The gun was by my ear. "If anybody breathes, he gets it."

The Step came down the path, calling weakly. Any other time I'd have laughed: he sounded pitiful. I knew how it would have been. When Mum found I was gone she'd have panicked. He'd have tried to soothe her: "Don't worry. It'll be some girl." Har har. Something like that. Then she'd have nagged and nagged him till he said, "All right. I'll go and search." His heart wasn't in it, you could hear. The wonder was he didn't hear *our* hearts thumping, in the bushes, an arm's reach away. "Todd?" the Step called. I opened my mouth, took a breath. Skinner cramped a hand across my face. I could only just breathe.

In the middle of the bridge, the Step came to a halt. He stopped calling. I could hear the *Oh*! as he realized what he'd just kicked with his foot. He stooped down and, at arm's length, as if it might bite, picked up the anorak. Saw it was mine. Saw the ripped arm dangling. "Oh, my God!" Then he was running back up the footpath. I heard his footsteps fading, and a crash of thunder, and the hammering of rain. But everything was fading. Skinner relaxed his grip a little, just enough to catch me as I passed out cold.

2 5 .

Darkness, heavy and thick all round me. Silence. Oily waters closing in. Deep silt and mud at the bottom, with secrets in it, litter, junk and the bones of little drowned things. There's a pain in my arm, a pain so bad I'm tempted to let the waters tuck me in and sleep, sleep, sleep.

There's a human voice, calling: Toddtoddtodd . . . A meaningless sound, but it reminds me of something. Something I was hunting for.

With an effort I stretch; my arms are long, long, reaching upwards, clutching. Finding something to hold onto. It's a rough but slimy wall.

I can handle this. My fingers are long and strong. My toes are just the same. I'm built for a life in the trees. I hang and swing as easy as breathing. And I run, too. The blood in my long legs tells me: hunt hunt hunt.

I know I'm hurt. I can feel my strength leaking away through the wound in my shoulder. But I claw my way up. With a wrench I pull free of the water that dribbles behind me. Then I slump on the canal side in a dripping heap.

I breathe the air. There's a blood smell on it. That reminds me. Hunger prods me upright, onto all fours, and I slide into the shadows, following my instincts, led by sound and scent. My teeth are tingling for a kill.

★   ★   ★

"Sssssscoming . . . " I groaned. That's what they told me, later. I thought I was being perfectly clear.

"Shut it," said Skinner.

"The boy's fainted," said Mister Multiplex. "Let him breathe."

Skinner eased his grip slightly. Sly said: "Listen. What's he saying?"

"Sssssscoming ... Sssssalive ... "

I looked round. Thank God, I was human. But there was something very near us. I could smell it in the air. "It's alive," I said. "The gog. It's coming. Get us out of here."

"Come off it," Skinner hissed. "If you think I'm falling for an old trick like that ... " Then the bush exploded round us in a splintering, crackling rush. There was panting and slavering and that sharp rank smell. As Skinner looked up, the gog hit him full on and the two of them rolled backwards over me. The dibbon shrieked. Multiplex had grabbed it in his arms and was backing away towards the fence. The poor thing thrashed and squealed. Sly grabbed my hand and yanked me with her. "Run!"

The gun cracked. The gog staggered sideways but it didn't drop. I caught a glimpse of Skinner with blood on his face and his eyes like a wild thing's. Then he leaped towards the van. I couldn't see much. My glasses were back there trampled somewhere and the rain slapped in my face. But I heard the door slam and the engine revved and whined. With a lunge the gog was on the bonnet, beating at the windscreen with bare hands. The engine roared, the wheels were skidding, spattering mud, but somehow the van didn't move. "Don't hang around. I let the tyres down," whispered Sly.

We knew that the gog was intelligent, but I wouldn't

have guessed what came next. It slipped down from the bonnet, almost thoughtfully, and scooped up a large stone from the grass verge. Then it smashed the windscreen – crack, crackle, shatter – in three blows. I'm glad I couldn't see the next bit, but I heard its howl, and Skinner's scream.

Sly was first through the gap beneath the fence, holding it up for Multiplex, then me. He was well on his way to the warehouse, almost hidden by the rain, and I was crouched down in the mud when there came one last bang from the van. All the noise of the fight stopped together.

"Quickly," Sly hissed. But I had to look. My arms and legs went weak, scrabbling feebly in the mud and the wire seemed to snag me and hold me tight. Slowly, something dragged itself back through the shattered windscreen, teetered there a moment, then turned to gaze down at me. The gog. Me. Eye to eye. So this was it, at last, the bad thing, the worst of all possible worlds. The eyes that held mine were deep-set, black-brown, glistening and sad, sad, sad.

It hauled itself towards me, one pace at a time. It was gasping and something dark was dripping through the teeth that made a kind of grin. Sly was tugging behind me, but I couldn't help her. I just stared. One of the gog's great arms was dangling, wounded. The other reached down slowly, as if I was something strange and monstrous, and just before it killed me, it wanted to understand.

26.

There was a gibbering wail. As its claw brushed my face, the gog looked up. Beyond the wire the dibbon shrieked a greeting to its long-lost other half. The gog felt the call. With a shuddering leap it was scaling the fence. Sly threw herself flat as it vaulted straight over her, landed with a painful thud and was running in long limping strides across the waste ground. With the one and only savage moment in its life, the dibbon sank its teeth in Multiplex's finger. Just for a moment, it turned big eyes, all sorry-sorry, up at him, then with a rubbery shrug it tore free from its maker's embrace and was racing through the rain to meet its brother. There was nothing anyone could do but stand and stare.

As they met, the dibbon stood up on its hind legs, quivering, to its full small height. The gog stopped, and its jaws came open in that dog-fanged grin. And then it sang. Not a howl or a roar, but a soft deep-down throaty note that made me think of a really old Blues record Dad had played me once. There was the same hiss and crackle in it, the same feeling that it came from far, far, far away. *An eighty-year-old woman sang that*, Dad had told me. *She was born a slave*.

At the sound, the dibbon yelped and chittered. Even Sly breathed, "Look ... " "A reunion ... " I said. That's when the gog hauled itself up – only to its knees, but still enough to bulk high above the other – and leaped. With a snarl of pure hate and disgust it hurled itself down on it, ripping and slashing with all its claws and teeth. It went on for maybe a minute. Then the big one crumpled, gave a last twitch and lay still. In the stillness that followed I noticed, through the rain, a faint blue flicker played on the end wall of the houses, where the street ran out.

When Sly and I reached Multiplex he did not speak. His long strand of hair had slipped off the bald patch long ago, and dangled over his left ear like a dreadful scar. He could have turned to stone – a gargoyle on a church roof, looking down on life, appalled.

"I'm a fool," he said quietly. "A fool. I should have known."

"What happened?" I said. "Why . . . ?"

He turned to me. "Don't you understand at all? The small one *loved* the other. What else could the big one do but hate?" Behind us, torches started moving down the footpath, frisking bushes as they went. "It might have escaped. Or killed you. But there was something it wanted even *more*. As soon as it saw its other half, all soft and silly, it loathed it. It had to destroy it, don't you see?" He came up close. "You do see, don't you? You two know – we all know – how that feels."

"Look." Sly was crouching near the bodies . . . not too near. "It's not dead, the big one."

The gog's sharp dog-toothed muzzle jerked; Sly jumped back. The rest of its body was a wet sack, soaking up the rain. Only the head strained a little to and fro. "It's in pain," Sly said. "Put it out of its misery." She was looking at me.

"Me? Why me?" I turned to Multiplex, but all he did was nod. He pointed to a plank that must have fallen from the catwalk.

"Quick," Sly said. "They're coming. Finish it." The plank was heavy, cold and slimy to the touch. I hoisted it up axe-wise. As I took a step towards the gog, it stirred. Sly hissed, "Now!" Out by the gate there were voices, and the rattling of a chain. A dog began to bark and bark. I slammed the plank down. And again.

I felt a warm hand on my shoulder. I thought I felt it trembling, but it might have been me. "Good man," said Multiplex. "Good man. Now, go tell the police. Tell them anything you like. Just ... give me enough time."

"To do what?" Sly said.

"What you said: turn them back." He caught my glance. "Yes," he said, "I can, I know it. You see, this is the end. Absolute fiasco, nothing left to lose. That's when the power comes. I can feel it. I could do ... *anything* now."

"Don't know about Todd," Sly said. "But I'm coming with you." He shook his head, but Sly took no notice. "Well?" she said to me.

I shrugged, sort of sheepish. "Like the man said, *nothing left to lose.*"

27.

He and I dragged the damp weight of the gog; it smelt sour now, slowly cooling. Sly pulled what was left of the dibbon, doing her best not to look. Inside the warehouse, we dumped them in the lift cage with a sick thump. There was a clang as the steel door shut behind us, and a bolt rasped in place.

"What now?" said Sly's voice in the dark.

"You two get out. You know the secret way."

"What about you?"

"Never mind me ... "

"You can't stay here," I said.

His hand clasped mine. I felt him reaching in the dark, like a blind man, till he found Sly's too. "Thank you," he said. "But I must. These things are part of me. I'll change them back, if time permits ... "

Three huge echoing clangs on the steel door drowned him. A megaphone crackled. *"Open up if you can hear me. This is the police."*

"And if not?" whispered Sly. "If you *don't* have time?"

"If not, better that they don't find anything at all. The world is full of men like Skinner. I swore he'd never get his hands on my ... my creatures. No ... " He squeezed our arms. "Don't argue. Understand. And *go.*"

Sly and I spoke, together: "Go where?"

"Well, home, of course."

Home? I thought. *What's that?* Sly gave a little hard

laugh. "Home!" Far off, and getting close, there was a multiple hee-haw of police sirens. A hard white light pried through the crack beneath the door.

"You've got homes," Multiplex's whisper trembled slightly. "Go to them." Neither of us moved.

"What if we don't want to?" I said.

His voice was gentler than I'd ever heard it. "What is it, Todd? Are your parents ... cruel to you?"

"No, no. It isn't them. I just don't want to go back to ... to being *me*."

The megaphone coughed. *"We know you're in there."* There was a pause. *"We have reason to think you are holding the boy, Todd. Bring him to the door now and you won't be harmed."*

"You're all right," said Sly. "You're brainy. Couple of years, all this'll be a story you tell your mates at college."

"You'll be all right," I said. "You know what to do. If I was half as smart ... as *brave*, as you ... "

"You *wha-a-a-t?*"

"Stop it!" Multiplex snapped. "Stop it, stop it. There isn't much time." He was only a voice, but soft and urgent now. "I understand. Oh yes ... only I was on my own with it. I never had someone else, someone who matched ... You do."

"Hold on," said Sly. "We don't even *like* each other."

"Of course you don't. You're opposites. Gog and dibbon. But listen to me." I felt the sweat of his palms; he was struggling with something. Outside, there was a scuffling, a panting, one bark, quickly hushed. They had our scent. "There's something I could do for you."

"You couldn't," Sly said.

I said, "You told us you never would. Not with people, you said. Never . . . Could you?"

"Yes," he said. "I'm certain of it. Just this once. It's all there is." His voice was firm now. The failed clown, the duff actor, the old-womanish little man was gone. In the light through the crack of the door I saw his profile, like an Easter Island statue staring out to sea.

"Trust me," he said. "There's no good reason why you should, of course . . . unless you're desperate."

"*This is your last chance.*"

The voice of the megaphone, louder this time, made the chambers of the warehouse ring. "*Repeat: your last chance. The boy's parents are willing to consider a ransom. Please make your demands . . .* " There was a squeal of feedback. "*We'll give you five minutes. We have oxy-acetylene cutters, and our officers are armed. Five minutes. Then we're coming in.*"

"What've we got to do?" said Sly.

"Do? Nothing. Try not to *think* at all. Just go on *wanting* what you want. All the things you envy, all the things you'd like to be . . . " His palm was resting on the back of my head, with a slight massaging motion. All the tension and the doubt began to drain away. "Or just think of each other. And one other thing . . . Trust me."

2 8 .

At first there was nothing, just the darkness of some inner corner of the warehouse. Mister Multiplex laid one hand on the back of Sly's head, one on mine. I've read about hypnosis. It was nothing like that.

The first thing was the prickling on my skin. All over, it was, as if I'd been dunked in fizzy lemonade. Then came the sounds – a buzzing, a rushing, a ringing not just in the ears but in my bones. It was like a stationary switchback ride. I was like a street where all the burglar bells and car alarms were going off at the same time, and a traffic jam was hooting and a Salvation Army brass band was marching past and kids with ghetto blasters were rushing through the crowd. It was like a party starting, like a carnival, with party poppers going off and fireworks whooshing and bursting and all the church bells clanging, wild and out of tune. That's when it really started. You know that moment when you switch a TV off, and the picture shrinks into a point of bright light, then *pings* out. Imagine that backwards. Imagine what came rushing into light, like the end of a tunnel when you're on an InterCity 125, wasn't just a picture on the screen but ... everything.

I wasn't in a warehouse any more. I wasn't sitting on a stone floor, wet and shivering. I was in a jostling market square. It was nowhere I knew, except the buildings all had that something about them – a bell-tower here, a minaret there – I could have sworn I'd seen somewhere before. On a hillside high above us huge white letters spelled out WEL-COME TO THE PLEXING PLANE like the Hollywood sign.

There must have been a fair in town. Before I could look at anything closely, the crowd heaved, carrying me with it. In one spot it cleared: a troupe of acrobats and jugglers were building a pile of themselves. There seemed to be too many heads for the number of bodies. They were juggling spare heads, six at a time, from one hand to the shoulders to the other hand and round again. Then they'd *hoopla*! and the pile disintegrated into cartwheels, landing with all their arms and legs assembled in a different order and with different faces smiling all the time.

There were sideshows. Swept past the Hall of Mirrors, I caught a glimpse of myself stretched thin as a liquorice stick, then one of me puffed out like bubblegum. "Roll up, roll up," went a barker with a real dog's head and a neat tail like a husky. "Have your passport photos taken here." He patted an old-fashioned camera, pointing at a board with painted figures and black holes where the faces ought to be. People queued up to be snapped as a family at the seaside – the kid with bucket and spade and demon horns and tail, the mum who was a mermaid or the dad with flowery boxer shorts and knobbly knees. Different faces kept poking through the dad hole, and a few of them I knew. The Step forced his whole head through and I left him there shouting for help because it was stuck.

There was a hot smell of animals suddenly, and a sign: MENAGERIE. A gryphon battered the bars of its cage with its lion hind-claws, then folded its eagle wings and clacked its beak. A couple of centaurs sulked in a pen of dirty straw. It had never occurred to me before that even fabulous animals would need mucking out. Something whistled and I turned to glimpse Einstein's Cheetah. I'd have recognized it anywhere.

It was much like the real-world kind of cheetah, but even at rest its outline was a kind of blur. Only its eyes were straight-ahead and certain, as they turned to look at me. I wanted it to be friendly. To thank me for inventing it. It didn't move. I realized then: there's always been an Einstein's Cheetah on the Plexing Plane. I don't know what it saw when it saw me.

The crowd gave a lurch and threw me forward. In the cleared space there was just me and another figure – Sly.

"Ladeeeeez and gentlemen . . . " A voice boomed. "Pray silence for the trick of all time." A snare drum rolled. "Please welcome ... MISTER MULTIPLEX!" He stepped out between us, from nowhere. He was wearing a sequin-spangled waistcoat and a bow tie and a top hat and he looked – how can I put it tactfully? – ridiculous.

"Don't take any notice of all this," he said quietly. "Think of each other." So I looked at Sly, and Sly looked at me. She wasn't the same, not quite, and she was changing. Not so short or slouching. Not so pudgy in the face, or maybe it was me. She'd got some of my lankiness, some of my bony angles, just enough to smooth her out. She was becoming elegant. I felt more compact, less as if there was always the odd six inches too much of me. With the palms of his hand on our heads, Mister Multiplex eased us gently towards each other. Any moment we would touch, and then ...

"Todd?" said a voice that wasn't quite hers. It was easy now. I only had to answer, "Sly."

Wasn't this what we wanted? To stop being odd-ones-out all our lives? To pick 'n' mix till we were normal, nothing special, neutralized? I said, "No."

The crowd roared as if at a missed goal; the menagerie exploded in cackles and screams; beasts broke free. The brass band struck up and the church bells started in again. The brilliant light of the Plexing Plane crumpled inwards, shrinking away to a dot in the darkness. Whined. And winked out.

I'd said NO.

29.

There was a crackling and a trail of sparks. Something cut the darkness like a comet tail. I was up in one jump but my legs wouldn't follow me, like when you try to leap straight out of sleep because you're late for school. My knees folded and cracked against the cold floor of the warehouse. The "No!" I was shouting came out as a groan.

I was here. In the real world. Damp and shivering, with police with metal cutters at the door. It gave way with a metallic clunk. The sparks puttered out, leaving ghosts of them, shoals of them, swimming in my vision. "Todd?" It was Sly's voice nearby, bleary. "We were ... *almost there...*"

"I'm sorry," I said. "You ... " I stopped. There was a sound I'd never thought I'd hear: Sly sobbing like a little child. Then the steel door raked open, and snow-blinding light slapped in. "Don't shoot," I called. "It's only us."

I was shielding my eyes, but people moved, and metal clanked, behind the light. "*Todd Whittington?*" said the megaphone voice and I heard Mum out there, "Yes, that's him."

"*Is anyone in there with you?*"

I looked round. Only the corners were dark; their shadows were deeper, if anything, now the warehouse had been stormed by artificial light. I spoke as slow and clearly as I could. "Yes. Just a friend. Sally Ann ... " I staggered upright and offered her my arm. She used me to get upright, then shook herself free.

I knew what to do. "He got away. He left us here." All this time we were staggering doorwards, with Sly pushing me feebly away, then grabbing onto me as she almost fell. Several figures moved forward of the spotlights, their long shadows closed like bars around us and we made our way to meet them at the door. It felt like walking uphill, but we had to make ground. We were making a space behind us where, if he had sense, if he had anything at all left in him, Mister Multiplex could get away.

There was a clink, and a rattly whirr in the warehouse behind us. The lift. He'd made it that far. The first policeman tensed. "What's that? You said there was no-one ... "

I couldn't think of an answer. I'd run out of bright ideas. I did the only thing I could think of, and maybe I'd have done it anyway. I passed out.

★   ★   ★

"You're all right, dear. You're safe."

Oh Mum, Mum, won't you ever learn? When you say things like that, with that let's-not-panic look in your eyes, I know there's trouble. What was the trouble now?

It started coming back to me. Creatures. Sly, Multiplex. And ... no, I thought, don't let me remember what happened to Skinner, please.

Then there was another thought, almost worst; it said: *it'll all have been a dream.* But it wasn't. I was in an ambulance. Mum was bending close over me, a bit too close, but I could still see the policeman just behind her and behind him, trying to get into the action somehow, the Step.

"Where's Sly?" I said.

"Who? Oh, the girl. She looks tough enough."

"Is she all right?"

"Yes, yes, they got you out in time."

"Out? Out of what?"

"It's nothing to worry about. There was some kind of explosion, and a fire."

"Fire?" I couldn't stop the questions coming. "In the warehouse? Did they find . . . ?" The words stuck there. The policeman looked at me closely, then at Mum, then me again.

"Completely gutted," he said. "Can't get near it. There'll be things we want to know." He frowned a moment. "What d'you mean: Did they find . . . what?"

Suddenly the Step had wriggled past him and was shielding me. "I suggest we let the boy sleep," he said. "You can see he's in shock."

The policeman wasn't backing off, not yet. "It's an ugly business, this, sir. If you'd seen that van . . . "

"That's enough," the Step said firmly. "Todd will help you all he can . . . when he's ready."

He's all right, the Step. I didn't forget that he *had* come looking for me, too. If he'd just get his dander up a bit more often, and stand up for himself, especially at home – I yawned, vaguely remembering a place called "home" – if he could, we might get to be friends.

30.

"I never finished what I was saying," I said. "In the warehouse, you remember ... "

Sly didn't turn round. Her fingers hooked into the wire links of the fencing round the burnt-out warehouse walls. "Are you listening?" I said. She didn't move.

I gave the fence a good hard rattle. "Ow!" She span round, ready to spit.

"Listen," I shouted. "I was only going to say: I didn't go through with the plexing because ... because ... *I liked you as you are.*"

She turned back to the fence, pressing her face close to it, her hair flopping forward, so I couldn't see. Only her knuckles tightened, going bloodless, as if she might tear the fence with her bare hands. "Big deal," she said. "What good's that? *I* don't like me, that's what counts."

"He liked you, too," I said, and for a while we both gazed over at the ruins. There was still a burnt wet ashy smell, days later, in the air. The fence had been patched and topped off with a shiny spool of razor wire, and a police car still nosed down here, at least once a day. The van had been towed off pretty quickly, before rumours spread. The story on the local news said Skinner's gun had gone off in the driver's seat. The story on the local grapevine talked about Rottweilers, poltergeists and the South African secret police; also that he'd be needing plastic surgery when he came out of Intensive Care. I guessed that last bit might be true.

Sly laughed, sourly. "Yeah, the old man liked me. So did the dibbon. Stupid thing."

"Sly, we'd just have been *normal*."

"Normal!" She sighed. "Tell that to the police. You know they want . . . *reports* on me."

"Mum's sending me to see a counsellor," I said. "Post-traumatic stress, you know."

"Waste of money," Sly gave half a smile. "You're no nuttier now than you always were." We smiled, for a moment.

"Sly . . . " I said. This was the bit I didn't fancy. I'd been practising all night. She must have sensed something in my voice, because she turned to face me. She looked younger, sort of eager, sort of shy.

"Sly, we're moving away."

"Oh." The curtains of her hair came down over her face again.

"I don't want to," I said. "I'd rather be here, but . . . " I felt limp again. "It's just for a few years," I said. "I'll leave home. And it's not that far to . . . "

"Bracknell," Sly said.

" . . . Bracknell. The counsellor says I need to see my dad sometimes. Hey, you said 'Bracknell' before I did. How did you know?"

She screwed her face up. "Dunno. It just came to me."

"I'll write," I said.

"Fat chance," said Sly. "Not me."

"You will," I said. "Good luck with the Teach Yourself Spelling."

She flushed red. "Who told you . . . ?"

"No-one," I said. "I just knew." We stared at each other. "Sly, are you thinking what I'm thinking ... ?"

"I think I am. Bits of it, anyway."

"Do you think the plexing ... sort of left a bit of each of us behind?"

"Dunno. Do it again."

"How?"

"Concentrate. Or something. I'll guess."

We both shut our eyes, and for a moment the whole wasteground quivered with our concentration. "Well?" I said.

She had both fists bunched at her temples as if she might beat her way in. Then she dropped them. "Nothing."

I shrugged. "Nothing ... I know one thing, though."

"What's that?"

"I won't forget you."

"You've done it again. That's what I was thinking too."

"Oh, another thing," I said, at the end of the street. I could see Mum waving, next to the removal van. She could wait. "I had one of my dreams. The spooky ones."

"The gog again?"

"No, Multiplex. I dreamed I saw him in the warehouse. Flames all round him. He had both hands up, like this ... like when he plexed us, but he'd worked out how to do it to himself." I shut my eyes, trying to remember. "He was turning into ... something. Then he'd break free."

"Something? What?"

"Don't know. I woke up."

"Typical!" she said. She looked me up and down. "You *would*."